"What do you need?" The whisper on her lips was like the finest drug.

What did he need? Onyx suddenly needed to taste the stranger more than he needed anything, more than he'd ever needed anything, including air.

He didn't have the words for that. Couldn't find a way to speak them, so instead, he lowered his head, and touched his mouth to hers.

"I need this," he said, his voice rough, a stranger's. "I don't need to know who you are, I don't need to ever see you again. But I need..."

She nodded, his strange woman, gripped his face again and stretched up on her toes, and still he had to lean down to meet her. Kissing her, gathering her up in his arms and pressing her petite frame to his body. It was like fire. It was like nothing he'd ever experienced before.

THE KING'S UNTIL MIDNIGHT

MILLIE ADAMS

PRESENTS

ISBN-13: 978-1-335-21392-1

The King's Until Midnight

Copyright © 2026 by Millie Adams

Harlequin Enterprises ULC
22 Adelaide St. West, 41st Floor
Toronto, Ontario M5H 4E3, Canada
www.Harlequin.com

HarperCollins Publishers
Macken House, 39/40 Mayor Street Upper,
Dublin 1, D01 C9W8, Ireland
www.HarperCollins.com

Printed in Lithuania

1 2 3 4 5 6 7 8 9 10 LIT 28 27 26 25

Millie Adams is the very dramatic pseudonym of
New York Times bestselling author Maisey Yates. Happiest
surrounded by yarn, her family and the small woodland
creatures she calls pets, she lives in a small house on the
edge of the woods, which allows her to escape in the way
she loves best—in the pages of a book. She loves intense
alpha heroes and the women who dare to go toe-to-toe
with them.

Books by Millie Adams

Harlequin Presents

Her Impossible Boss's Baby
Italian's Christmas Acquisition
His Highness's Diamond Decree
After-Hours Heir
Dragos's Broken Vows
Promoted to Boss's Wife
Heir of Scandal
From Convent to Queen

Work Wives to Billionaires' Wives

Billionaire's Bride Bargain

Young, Hot and Royal

Princess, Pregnant, Prisoner
King's Captive Bride

Visit the Author Profile page
at Harlequin.com for more titles.

CHAPTER ONE

King Onyx of Basilia was no stranger to the cruelty of life. That it was unjust and often took people far before their time was nothing new to him.

Death might be inevitable, but it was no less shocking.

No matter how degraded his relationship with his wife had been, to lose her to a sudden medical event two days prior, and to have already buried her today was still a pain that overtook his entire body.

It was a tangle of guilt and sadness that he wasn't sure if he would ever be able to fully undo.

There was no fixing anything, not now. Any hope he'd had that he and Circe could fix their fractured marriage was dead now. Along with his wife.

In the blink of an eye, everything was changed. Gone. Everything.

They'd been intent on trying for a child, on improving things between them.

It was the promise of an entire future, wiped away, and the unrelenting pain that he felt over that was more than he had ever imagined.

And yet at the same time, the hardest part of his life was now erased, and that felt cruel to even think.

He tightened his hand into a fist and turned away from the roaring fireplace looking around the dimly lit, desolate library.

He was, now and always, a king before he was anything else. He couldn't give in to this strange, sinking despair in his chest that also wound itself around a feeling of...*freedom*.

There was no freedom. A woman was dead. His wife was dead. The future of the kingdom now in turmoil.

He could see Circe as she'd been, magnetic and angry and distant, smart and prickly and alive.

What a waste.

What a terrible, tragic waste. That much he did believe. Deeply in his soul. Because for all that he and Circe hadn't even liked each other in the end, she had been a vibrant woman.

Well-liked by the people for her fiery ideals and opinions, for her beauty and her sense of fashion and fun.

Onyx and Circe had found it difficult to communicate with each other, to put it mildly. There hadn't been a spark between them, nothing to even make the growing bitterness between them exciting. At least if there had been a spark they might've found compatibility in bed. But no. Circe made it clear she didn't enjoy sex with him, rebuffing him more often than she accepted his advances, and he could understand it.

They were emotionally distant. While he'd longed to try to find some closeness in the bedroom, she'd needed the closeness to even begin. But she'd never wanted that closeness either.

He hadn't wanted a divorce. That kind of scandal was antithetical to what he wanted to bring to Basilia.

He wanted to be like his father.

A man who had done right by his country and his family until his very last breath.

What did right even look like now? He wished he had his father with him so that he could ask. So he could have asked him when a convenient marriage should begin to turn to love, or at least like. So he could have seen what his parents' marriage looked like later, and asked about the changing nature of love, of duty.

He stood there, his jaw clenched.

The truth was, Circe had been an honorable queen who had helped him with what he wanted even when they didn't mesh.

In spite of the difficulty in their marriage, she had stayed. She had agreed to give him his heir. They'd been discussing methods, and had decided to go with in vitro to give them the best chance. She'd been on hormones and he'd felt a deep anguish that maybe that had caused the aneurysm. After all, it was the only thing that had changed.

The doctor assured him that wasn't the reason but he had trouble believing it. Then, he had no clarity at all. He had nothing but a pain that sat at the center of his chest howling.

Guilt. Relief. Anger. Denial. Stages of grief that he'd never even seen listed, winding themselves around each other and moving in and out of order.

He kept trying to wake up. From this wretched nightmare. From this horrendous thing he didn't know how to navigate. He couldn't.

One night he'd gone to bed a teenage boy with nothing more pressing on his mind than driving his new car, the crush he had on an adviser's daughter, the pressing concern about when and how he might lose his virginity, and he'd woken up a king.

This reminded him of that singular, altering moment in his life.

That his life was forever changed in the space of one breath.

He no longer had Circe in the palace, or in his life; for all that it had been challenging, it had been something. The lack of her left a cavern behind.

The funeral had been beautiful and well attended. There were many guests staying in the palace in the aftermath of it. Diplomats and dignitaries from all over the island, minor royals, politicians and celebrities from countries far and wide.

And as always his sister, Emerald, was here, along with her husband, Andrei, who was also the head of Onyx's guard.

If he wanted to sit and take comfort in friends, he could.

And yet in this moment he wanted only solitude.

Craved it.

So when he heard the door open, tension washed through him. He turned and squinted into the darkness.

Just as a small figure slipped into the room, blond hair in a tumble, her face obscured in the dim light. She was dressed in black, as all the guests had been. As he was.

She looked up, but he still couldn't make out her features. "Oh. Your Highness. I'm sorry."

"No need to apologize," he said. "I can take my leave."

He moved away from the fireplace, and the woman moved nearer to him. Her movements tentative.

"I'm sorry," she said.

This was a different apology to the first. That had been about her worry she'd interrupted him. This was different.

Her voice was low and husky. A function, perhaps of the fact that she was trying to keep quiet in the stillness of the room.

He couldn't see her expression, but he could hear the earnestness in her voice. A sweetness he'd not heard from anyone else. A sincerity that felt unique. "I know that it's been said to you a hundred times. But I would say it a hundred more. I'm… I'm so very sorry for your loss."

It *had* been said to him. A hundred times was perhaps understating it. He'd been wrestling with it for days. Circe's parents, her sisters and brother, deserved sympathy far more than he did. They knew her. In many ways, Onyx knew he'd never scratched the surface of her, and perhaps doing so wouldn't have fixed anything.

But this felt different. It felt like something he could accept. It felt like sympathy that was somehow created for him, and matched him in a way he couldn't explain. It was balm for him in the moment.

She was small, this woman, short, petite and very slim. She moved closer to him, the top of her head barely reaching his chest. An emotion too large for him to name began to grow at the center of his chest. A bitter regret that was something other than grief.

The woman lifted her hand and touched his face. Everything in him went still. This was the first time he'd been touched by someone other than his family for at least two years. That part of his marriage to Circe had been resolutely dead even before she'd gone. What they'd been trying to keep intact was a partnership for the sake of the country.

The idea of there being any sort of romance between them long gone.

That futile hope he'd had as a young man when he'd taken her as his wife—

Perhaps that was the source of the shameful relief that he'd felt. This sense of being free that made him feel an enormous streak of guilt.

He was a man.

He had been nothing but a king, a husband whose wife recoiled at his touch, for so many years, and now this woman's hands were on his face reminding him that beneath all of that, he was a man.

This woman that he couldn't even see clearly.

Her blond hair was curly, the firelight making a halo around her, her features obscured. He didn't know her. If she was someone that he knew then she would've been recognizable even in this light.

The black dress she was wearing clung to her petite curves, her breasts small, but pert, her hips delicate.

He was trying to remember all of the people that had been at the funeral.

Who she might be with. Where she might be from. There was a delicate air of aristocracy around her; that much was certain. She could be a celebrity, but more likely she was a dignitary, political figure or someone of social prominence.

And allowing her to touch him in this way was a risk. As much of a risk as it was wrong.

What man would experience lust for another woman two days after his wife died? It was abhorrent. And yet he didn't want her to stop touching him. Likely she only meant it as a comfort, but it was making his blood warm. Making it stir.

It was making him feel things that he'd decided were best left dead.

He felt hungry then. Hungry for the kind of connection he hadn't experienced in so long. Maybe ever. This woman's sweet touch, this simple condolence warmed him in parts of himself that he'd thought were long dead.

But it was only that. Just an act of comfort. Still, he stood frozen, letting her touch him like that, until that touch shifted, just slightly, and there was a change in the way that she was breathing. More ragged, more labored.

He could feel his own heart raging, his body responding to this.

Then the little woman in front of him lifted another hand, touched the other side of his face, holding him now. He couldn't make out the color of her eyes, not in this light. Couldn't make out the fine details of her features. But he knew that she was beautiful. "I'm so sorry," she whispered. She stretched up on her toes and kissed his cheek.

Then she began to pull away, and he reached back, cupping the back of her head, her hair sliding through his fingers, silken and tempting.

What in God's name was he doing?

Nothing in God's name—that much was certain.

This was Eros. It was Hades. It was all things wrong and sweet and tempting. Nothing he'd ever indulged in.

But he couldn't let her move away from him.

She smelled of lilacs and of need. Of everything that he had been afraid of these past years. Afraid to miss, afraid to want.

His parents had married for duty, and within that, they'd found love. He had truly believed that he might find that for himself. He hadn't. Instead, what he had proved was that marrying a stranger could be nothing but an absolute disaster if the two people were incompatible. Years and years wouldn't fix it.

Nothing would fix it.

Nothing would fix *this*.

Nothing except the simple glide of her hair through his fingers felt like it was fixing something.

Made him feel more alive, more whole than anything ever had.

"What do you need?" The whisper on her lips was like the finest drug.

What did he need? He suddenly needed to taste the stranger more than he needed anything, more than he'd ever needed anything, including air.

He didn't have the words for that. Couldn't find a way to speak them, so instead, he lowered his head, and touched his mouth to hers. And for the first time in two years, he was kissing a woman.

For the first time in longer than he could remember, he was kissing one with true, real passion. Holding her head in his palm, he angled his own, parting his lips and sliding his tongue against hers. She made a short, whimpering sound, and moved away from him. He froze.

"I need this," he said, his voice rough, a stranger's. "I don't need to know who you are, I don't need to ever see you again. But I need…"

She nodded, his strange woman, gripped his face again and stretched up on her toes, and still he had to lean down to meet her. Kissing her, gathering her up in his arms and pressing her petite frame to his body. It was like fire. It was like nothing he'd ever experienced before.

Even before his marriage he hadn't been the kind of man to take strangers as lovers. He hadn't been indiscriminate with sex. He couldn't afford to be. He was a king. And he didn't trust nondisclosure agreements to that extent. Nor did he feel that a king should act in such a manner that it necessitated them. He had relationships. A couple, before he'd chosen Circe to be his queen. He'd imagined that they would have a reasonable sex life, but it had gone from bad to nonexistent in their five years of marriage and he was…hungry.

An experience that he'd never had before had presented itself to him, and he did not possess the ability to deny himself. She whimpered against his mouth, and he lifted her up off the floor, carrying her to the large chaise in the corner of the room. The room was much darker than he would've liked, but he didn't want to turn the lights on. He didn't want to do anything to break the spell of the moment. To feel like he was lifting the veil.

This was magic.

He was a man who'd experienced precious little magic in his life, and he wanted this. He didn't want to think about anything that had come before. Didn't want to think about the grief that sat at the center of his chest, didn't want to think about the future.

A future where he would have to find another queen. Where he would have to produce an heir. Where he would potentially fail as a husband all over again. Right now he wasn't failing. Right now, he had a warm, willing woman in his arms who was as into this as he was, and he wasn't going to release his hold on her.

Not for anything.

Nimble fingers began to work the buttons on his shirt, and he found it pushed off of his shoulders, and he assisted. Her palms were flat against his chest, and he could see that her eyes were wide, glittering as she moved her hands over his muscles, fingertips skimming his nipples, the sensation so erotic he grasped both of her wrists in one hand and held her still for just a moment. "I am on edge," he said.

"Did I do something wrong?" she whispered.

"No," he growled. "It's too good. Too good. I don't want to lose control."

"I don't mind if you do," she whispered. "I told you. This is for you. Whatever you need."

If he were to discover that this was a hallucination, one brought about by the horrors of the last week, he would have been unsurprised. Because this seemed like something straight out of a dream he'd never allowed himself to have.

He released his hold on her, and she moved her fingers down his chest, his stomach, her touch reverent. Her dress was a stretchy, knit material, and he pushed it up her hips, peeling the clinging material away from her body, leaving her in dark-colored, brief underwear and a black bra. His blood was running hot and fast. Everything inside of him begging him to take her. Take her.

He was about to ask yet again if she was certain this was what she wanted, when her hands went to his belt buckle, undid the button and zipper on his pants. Her hands were trembling, and he lifted one up to his lips and kissed her fingers. "It doesn't have to—"

"I want this," she said.

It was the first time she had been very clear that she wanted more than simply to comfort him.

She was clear. She wanted this. She wanted *him*.

He needed to be wanted. He hadn't known that. Hadn't realized how hungry he was for someone to desire him. He was a confident man; he had every reason to be. But five years of being treated as if his desires were a punishment had taken something from him. Eroded like waves against sand, slowly stealing pieces of who he'd been before with each pass of the tide.

This was like being healed.

So he stripped off the rest of his clothes, reached behind her back and unsnapped her bra before moving down to slide her underwear down her legs.

He wished that he could see her better, and yet was grateful that he couldn't. Because there was no way he would be able to keep his control and his composure. Even now, in the dim light, the faint impression of her body was enough to make him come. It took digging deep into his self-control to keep from losing it.

He kissed her again, reaching down between her legs and feeling how wet she was. So wet. For him. And with ease. He moved his thumb over her clit, before pushing two fingers inside of her. She whimpered, moving her hips in time with his strokes.

He moved his mouth away from hers, kissed down her neck, down to her glorious breast, where he sucked one tight nipple into his mouth, the sensation making his cock pulse with need. He growled, grinding his hips down into hers, wrapping one arm around her waist and drawing her up against him as he flexed against her.

Her hands went to his hair, fingers digging into his scalp. He moved, and felt the head of his arousal right up against her slick entrance. He couldn't hold back. "Yes," she whispered in his ear.

All that he needed to hear.

He drove into her, the harsh cry on her lips fueling him on. She was so tight. So glorious and perfect.

It had never been like this. Not ever. He had never felt anything quite so essential. Had never felt like coming home before. But it did now.

He began to move, gripping both of her hips as he drove himself home, over and over again. Then he felt her begin to tighten around him, her back arched against him.

"Yes," he whispered. "Come for me, darling."

Her cries of pleasure seemed to shock her, her hand coming up and covering her own mouth as her internal muscles clenched around him, as she lost her control completely.

He couldn't hold on. Not any longer. He let himself go, claiming her hard and fast, until his need was a raging beast he could no longer outrun.

He growled, pouring himself deep inside of her, the pleasure blotting out everything. Every thought. Every pain. Every doubt. Everything. For one, blissful moment, he knew what it was to simply be a man. A man lost in need. A man perhaps found in need as well.

He kissed her. Deep, hard.

Wrapped her tightly in his arms, and felt sleep begin to drag him down, an exhaustion that he'd never felt before claiming his entire body.

When he awoke with a start, he was naked on the chaise lounge, alone. All signs of his beautiful partner gone.

He would've thought that he'd dreamed it if he weren't naked.

Still, he had a difficult time believing it had actually happened.

He didn't know her name. He didn't know who she was.

She had given him the most singular moment of his life, and now she was gone.

And he was left to deal with the aftermath of a life that was in ruin.

CHAPTER TWO

BIRDIE WAS TERRIFIED she was going to lose her job. She had no idea what she'd been thinking. Well, sadly she actually *did* know what she'd been thinking. Or at least, what she'd been feeling.

Onyx.

Oh, that man had a hold on her that surpassed reason and sense. He had from the first moment she'd seen him and then…

When she got up the next morning, and put on her pale blue uniform, she felt…different. Altered fundamentally. Changed.

She avoided her own reflection as she got ready. Didn't even look herself full in the face when she brushed her teeth. Until she couldn't stand it anymore.

She lifted her gaze and looked herself in the eyes.

Her blond hair was wild.

She looked… She did look different. Her cheeks had more color in them than she'd ever seen, her lips still looked bruised from kissing him.

The *king*.

Terror, desire and grief clenched her heart in a fist.

What was going to happen when she walked in today?

She showered, trying to ignore how sensitive her body felt, then stepped out and dried her hair as straight as possible, and ruthlessly pinned it back into the bun she wore every day at work. Well, every day but yesterday, when the staff had been asked to look nicer for the funeral.

She borrowed one of her stepsister's black dresses out of the back of her closet because she knew she'd never notice. Both of her stepsisters had so many different outfits from brand deals, and they usually only wore an outfit once.

She'd left her hair down and curly, and worn a dress much tighter and shorter than she normally would.

Now she was put back together. The woman she'd been last night successfully hidden beneath her loose-fitting uniform.

Still, she was very apparently her. What was he going to say?

There was really only one way to find out. But first, she had to run the gauntlet of her house.

This clattering old home, where she slept in the attic with one threadbare blanket and a mattress that could hardly be called that.

She sighed heavily and walked out the door, the noise of the day already blaring up the stairs.

"I'm filming a get-ready-with-me, get out of the frame."

"I have more followers than you. It would help you if I was in your video."

"Girls! Take turns filming."

She did her best to paste a smile on her face, because she didn't want to have a conversation with her stepmother, or her stepsisters. She just wanted to get to work. To her job, which paid for quite a lot of the bills around here, in spite of the fact that her stepsisters fancied themselves to be influencers.

It wasn't that she'd ever been thrilled with her stepfamily, but she'd been content with them as long as she'd believed her father was happy.

Her mother's death had destroyed him. He'd gone from being a chaotic ball of fun to being stressed constantly, perennial circles beneath his eyes as he tried to manage being a single father, and realizing his dreams for the future.

Then he'd had a windfall, he'd met her stepmother and he'd seemed very nearly like happy, and that was good enough for Birdie.

She tried to be happy and optimistic as much as possible. If for no other reason than that she knew her mom wanted her to live happily. Even dying, her own mother had held onto optimism, not false hope, but a kind of joy that made Birdie want to live with as much of it as possible.

That didn't mean it was easy.

After losing her mom everything had been different.

Day-to-day life had been easy if not idyllic when her father had been wealthy in cryptocurrency, but then it had collapsed suddenly overnight, giving him a heart attack and killing him with the stress of it, leaving her with her stepmother—a woman who considered herself nobility because of some specious relation to a minor British royal, and her stepsisters. All of whom felt that they were *above* doing actual jobs.

That was why Birdie had gotten work at the palace when she was seventeen.

Birdie's father had been a self-made man, one who had come up from nothing, and that made Birdie a commoner in the eyes of her stepmother.

That meant *she* was responsible for practical, steady work while her sisters focused on becoming niche internet microcelebrities.

If they knew what she'd done last night…

That made Birdie smile even more resolutely. She walked into the kitchen and saw Alana standing at the counter with a giant puffy headband holding her hair back, and a large light illuminating her face, her phone right in front of her.

"Don't walk into my shot," Alana said.

"I won't," said Birdie, deftly moving around her and making her way to the fridge to grab her sack lunch and a cup of yogurt.

"You got back late last night," her stepmother said, eyeing her closely.

"It was the queen's funeral," Birdie said, her chest getting so tight it was almost impossible for her to breathe. "We had a lot of extra work to do."

"Of course," she said. "I know that. But I assume that you have information about who is visiting. And about that *poor* man."

If there was one thing her stepmother was, it was fake. Asking after another person's well-being wasn't in her repertoire. "Do you mean…the king?" Birdie asked.

"Of course. This must be such a devastating loss for him!" Her pause was artful. Very nearly believable.

"But obviously he will have to marry again. He didn't have an heir."

Birdie's cheeks went hot. She didn't need to say anything. She didn't need to say anything. She didn't need—

"He's only just buried his wife. I don't think that it's the right time to talk about his next marriage."

Her stepmother narrowed her eyes, and Birdie took some satisfaction in watching all the places her Botox failed to keep her skin from wrinkling. "Don't talk like you know him, Roberta. You probably never even see him in that massive palace."

He's been inside me, actually.

She did *not* say that.

She also didn't tell her stepmother that she spoke to the king fairly regularly. She wished that she didn't. She wished that he were distant. Instead, at seventeen she'd been assigned work in his study. Often bringing him food when he was in there.

She wasn't his personal maid or anything like that, but during the day she was the one that attended him. Not that she'd ever shared that bit of information with her stepmother. Nor would she.

Developing a crush on him was easy. He was a beautiful man. His cheekbones high and well-formed, his eyes black like onyx, like his name, his mouth compelling. But he was also kind. Interesting. Funny, even. It wasn't like they had long conversations. It was just little exchanges here and there. But she'd fallen for him.

She might've felt guilty about being in love with a married man except it was honestly a lot like having a crush on a celebrity. Yes, she did see him, but he was as unreachable as he might've been if he were on the silver screen. At least, he had been. Until last night. It had all been too much for her to bear.

She'd walked into the room, just to get a little bit of solace after the overwhelming sadness of the funeral, of all the proceedings, and he'd been in there. All she'd wanted to do was comfort him.

But it was difficult to remove that from how much she wanted him. And then, when he kissed her...

She would've given him anything. She had given him everything.

It was her first time, and she couldn't have regretted it. How could she? He was the object of her deepest desires, and he needed her. But now she had to go to work and face him, and she didn't know how things would be different.

Combined with all of that, she simply couldn't bear her stepmother trying to scheme her ridiculous daughters into the palace.

"It doesn't matter whether I know him or not," she said. "His wife has been dead for three days. And if you had seen him at the funeral, then you would know how heartbroken he is."

That was the one thing that hurt. Last night, he could've easily been imagining that he was with the queen. Did she even have a right to feel hurt about that? She had moved in on a man who was grieving. He'd needed comfort, and she had provided that. But perhaps part of accepting that was accepting that it wasn't about her personally, no matter how much it had mattered to her.

"Keep your ear to the ground," her stepmother

said. "We need to know when he plans to take another queen, because you know he will. And you know he can't tarry."

The annoying thing was, it was true. He would have to produce an heir sooner rather than later. He was thirty, after all.

There was now a distressing mortality rate among the royalty in this country. His parents, the king and queen, had died when he'd been just sixteen. Birdie had been so young she didn't remember a time when anyone had been king except for him.

But now, his wife was gone. He'd have to find a new one. Though one thing her stepmother was wrong about was any inkling that she might have a hope in hell at marrying one of her daughters off to him.

Specious royal connections and internet fame did not a queen make.

Of course, Birdie didn't have a chance at all.

With hate in her heart, and a knot in her stomach, she got into her tiny, ramshackle car and drove to the palace.

Her hands were shaking when she got to the staff lot, and by the time she walked in she thought she was going to throw up.

Elizabeth saw her and grabbed her arm. "Are you okay?"

"I'm fine."

Birdie's own stepmother could not be called a mother figure, not in any capacity. But lovely Elizabeth had been a soft influence like Birdie had never known from the moment she'd started working at the palace three years earlier.

Her dark hair was streaked with gray, her blue eyes glimmering with good humor.

She always looked out for Birdie. In fact, Elizabeth was the reason that Birdie had ended up working in the king's study. She had thought that Birdie would be good for the job, and had worked to get her in even though she was inexperienced.

"You don't look okay. I think yesterday was taxing for you."

Of course it was. The man that she loved was going through an unimaginable pain, and Birdie had guilt-inducing, complicated feelings about it even without sleeping with him. The thing was, even though he wasn't married now, he was as off-limits as he'd ever been.

A king couldn't marry a maid.

The end.

No discussion.

The best thing she could hope for was to become a mistress. She wasn't really sure how she felt about that.

Well.

She had allowed him to take whatever liberties he wanted, and taken many of her own besides. So there was that.

There was also the fact that it was a horrible thing to be even remotely pleased by the vacancy the queen had left behind. She would never say that she was glad she was gone. That was absolutely horrendous.

"No more so than it was for anyone else. I'm fine."

"He's in his study already."

Birdie did her best not to react to that.

"I'll go check in on him."

"You're a good girl."

Birdie grimaced. Elizabeth wouldn't say that if she had any idea what had happened last night.

Birdie had no idea what it made her. Besides desperate.

Her mouth dry, she made her way to the king's study. Then she took a breath, and pushed the door open. He barely looked up at her.

"Good morning," he said.

Birdie stopped, her stomach clenched tight like someone had grabbed it, her heart leaping up into her throat. His head was bent over the newspaper he was reading, a dark lock of hair fallen over his forehead and her fingers itched to brush it back. He looked exhausted. The hollows of his cheekbones were more hollow than they had been a week ago. He had circles under his eyes.

She wanted to go to him. Sit on his lap and smooth those lines away. Feel him hot and hard beneath her, his arms around her.

She stood, frozen. And then he did look up. Their eyes met, and she felt like she'd been punched. "Could I get some coffee?"

She stood there, staring.

Oh God.

He didn't recognize her. He hadn't known who she was.

She served him every day, and he didn't know *who she was*.

Last night, it had been dim in the room, and while she would never mistake him for someone else, he simply didn't look at her close enough on a given day for her to be significant to him.

She had just been a woman. Any woman. Anybody. He had taken her because he needed comfort. He probably had been thinking of his wife.

You foolish girl. You foolish, stupid girl. Of course you don't mean anything to him.

He's never looked at you closely enough, all the times you've been in here serving him, all the times you thought you were having a moment, he never even looked at you closely enough to know who you were if you changed your clothes or your hair.

"Of course, Your Highness," she said.

On completely numb feet she stumbled out of the room, making her way toward the kitchen. She went past Elizabeth. "Birdie?"

She ignored her as she went to make coffee.

Well. There was one good thing about this. She wouldn't lose her job.

At least, that was what she thought. Because of course, he had no idea the two of them had slept together, so why would it matter?

And as the weeks passed, the ache in her chest didn't go away. And even worse, the cramps from her monthly didn't arrive.

There was no way. One time. Just one time.

But even still, she stopped at a drugstore far away from her house before she went home from work a month after the queen's funeral, and bought a test.

She couldn't risk taking it at home. So she drove from the convenience store to a coffeehouse she never went to, bought a drink and then slipped into the bathroom. She opened up the test and took it. Waiting for the results with bated breath.

It was positive.

She, Roberta Matthews, almost always called Birdie, maid at the palace, servant to a king, was pregnant with the heir to the throne of Basilia.

And the king didn't even know they'd slept together.

CHAPTER THREE

Four months later

"ARE YOU WELL?"

"Not especially," Onyx said, looking up at his friend and brother-in-law Andrei, who was standing at the other end of his study, staring at him.

Andrei was the head of his security, and had married Onyx's sister a year ago after her own convenient marriage imploded disastrously.

Well, Andrei was the one who had imploded the convenient marriage.

At the time, Onyx had been livid. His head of security had not acted in the best interest of the country, but rather his and Emerald's hearts. The two of them had been in love for years, but had always believed it impossible for them to be together. Now they had a child, and were deliriously happy in a way that Onyx had certainly never been.

Which made Andrei's inquiry now grate in a way that was perhaps unfair.

"What's this about?"

"I'm grieving," he snapped.

"I have no doubt you are," Andrei said, sounding unbothered. "But you and I both know it's more complicated than most people think. Remember, I lived here in the palace with you and your wife. I know you weren't in love with her."

"I won't lie and try to change history now, but do you honestly think that makes it easier?"

"From the perspective of guilt? No. I don't. From the perspective of missing her? I would assume so."

His brother-in-law was so madly in love with Emerald that he'd nearly toppled two governments to claim her. If he were to lose her… Onyx couldn't even think of it, because loss wasn't theoretical to him. It was far too real.

But he knew that Andrei wouldn't be mired in melancholy if he lost his wife. He'd likely burn the world down.

"I suppose that's true," Onyx said.

"Then what is bothering you?"

Did he tell him? He was his oldest friend. Though, there had been a big breach of trust around Emerald. It was the secrecy of it. The fact that Andrei hadn't come to him about his feelings for his sister. And then, when he'd kidnapped her from her wedding, he'd hidden her location even from Onyx. It wasn't that he was still angry with him about it, but it did make him feel like he didn't owe his friend an explanation.

But he felt that he might need to give it.

Five months on from the funeral. From when he'd made love to that woman. She was all he could think about. He craved her. Wanted her in his bed again more than he wanted anything else.

And he had no idea who she was or how to find her.

"I have something to tell you, and it will likely make you think ill of me."

Andrei shrugged. "That's fine. I've given you plenty of reasons to think ill of *me*."

Onyx had just been thinking of those reasons. He didn't say that.

"The night of Circe's funeral I…" He closed his eyes, gritting his teeth together. "There was a woman."

"Oh dear," Andrei said, moving closer to where Onyx sat.

"She came to me in the library. I… I don't know who it was. I didn't recognize her. It was dim and I didn't want to turn the lights on. I didn't want to think better of…what happened."

"I assume you slept with her."

"Yes."

He wouldn't do anything to malign Circe by saying how long it had been since the two of them had slept together. Andrei knew full well that the marriage was dysfunctional. He didn't need to do anything else to make him dislike a dead woman.

Andrei looked philosophical. "Well, you probably needed it."

He had. He'd needed it more than he'd ever needed anything in his life. Though admitting that felt shameful.

"It's not a bad thing to have feelings, Onyx," his friend pointed out.

"I know that," he said. "But it is not the way I would normally behave, and I'm not proud of myself."

"Don't be proud, then. But it happened. I'm no stranger to that."

"I know. Except when you lost control it was with my sister and you created an international incident."

"Congratulations on avoiding political upheaval with your ill-advised sex. You are right. I can't say the same." Andrei was, as ever, unrepentant.

"I want to find her," he said. "She's all I can think about. I have to get married again. And there's a woman out there… As long as she's not married to someone else, I need her to be mine. She must've been a guest at the funeral." His thoughts began to move faster. "I don't see why I can't take her to be my wife. I've never wanted anyone the way I wanted her."

"And how are you going to find her? You can hardly go around acting like Prince Charming, seeing who fits your cock, can you?"

Onyx almost laughed at that, an angry huffing sound working the back of his throat. "Hardly."

"So, you have to invite everyone back who was at the funeral. For a ball."

"Are you out of your damned mind? We can't have a party this soon after Circe's death."

"She loved a party," Andrei said. "Particularly one in her honor."

"I am especially not having a party in my dead wife's honor for me to find another woman."

"Why not? She didn't want you. She would probably be thrilled that you were moving on to somebody else. She would only wish that she was still alive to see it. I know that that makes things complicated. Because you're trying to present as a grieving husband for all the world to see, but you aren't. Not in the way that you would like to be. I want to see you happy. If you can find this woman, then you should do it. And not wait any longer."

"I didn't see her face," he said. "When I say I don't know who she was, I mean… I really don't know. She was small, and I'm almost totally certain blonde. Her hair was long and very curly, but women change their hair all the time."

Andrei seemed to consider that. "I can see how that's a problem."

"I'd have a better shot at recognizing her in the dark."

"A masquerade," Andrei said. "Have a masquerade. It's so dramatic that it's perfect. You'll see her as you did that night. Not fully revealed, and you'll have to find her again based on that connection you had with her."

"I don't know that desire can be called…connection."

Andrei snorted. "Lies. It is. It's only that you've never experienced it like this, am I right?"

He shook his head slowly. "No."

"I know you don't wish to hear too much about the way I feel about your sister. But I spent years trying to deny it. I spent years sleeping with women who looked like her, thinking to myself that I could demystify her. Take the edge off what I felt. But desire isn't about beauty. Yes, it's part of it, but there's more. There's something more that makes it so no one else will do, that no one else will truly satisfy you. That is what you'll recognize. I promise you."

The door to his study opened, and the little maid who saw to all of his needs during the day came in. She was such a funny, unassuming creature. Her blond hair always done in a tight bun, the pale blue uniform she wore making her figure an indistinct shape. She never met his gaze. She always scuttled around like she was nervous. When they spoke, he found her amusing. Which always surprised him because so much of her demeanor seemed bashful.

"Good morning," he said.

"Good morning, your highness," she said, edging around Andrei and setting a tray of tea and sweets on his desk.

He wanted to tell Andrei he was insane, but he also wanted this to work. He just needed to believe it could.

"And what?" he asked. "We send out repeat invites, and say all of you who came to the funeral, come to this masked ball now?"

"We can expand it. Include some of the ladies in the kingdom. We have a full list of people who came, and that can be repeated. So I think that's exactly what we should do. And actually, I know you feel it's quite early, but you should definitely find a wife at least a year before you take one. So even if you do meet someone at the ball, you can take your time. No one has to know what you're up to behind closed doors."

The maid dropped a teacup onto the floor, shattering the porcelain. "I'm sorry. I'm so sorry I…"

Something jolted inside him and he turned to look at her. His head was bent, she was on her knees cleaning up the glass and something…tugged at him.

I'm sorry. I'm so sorry.

His head swam with memories of the night, of the woman.

He was losing his senses. If a maid breaking a cup could even be a callback to that encounter then he knew he had to take action. No one liked a man who wallowed rather than acting.

He didn't even like himself at the moment.

"Don't worry," he said to the little creature scrambling to undo her mistake.

"I won't trouble you further," she said, clutching the pieces of cup in her hands and rushing from the room.

"Is she all right?" Andrei asked.

"I don't know. She's always jumpy."

"Well. I hope that you'll heed what I'm saying to you."

"Yes," he said. "You're not wrong. Nothing that you're saying is wrong. Even if it is annoying."

"I have a tendency to be like that. Ask your sister."

"I don't need to. I've seen evidence of this in my own life all too well."

"I think we need to do this," Andrei said. "I think it's the best thing we can do. For you, and for the country."

After all these months, he was still so hungry for her that his resolve was weak.

"All right. We will have a ball. And I will choose my new wife."

Birdie thought that her heart was going to gallop out of her chest, and worst of all, she thought she might pass out. She made it out of the study, and managed to get to the kitchen. She leaned against the wall next to the stove, trying to shrink into an alcove.

That was where Elizabeth found her.

She looked at her with sharp blue eyes. "Birdie," she said. "You and I are going to go into my quarters and have a talk."

Being the manager of the household staff, Elizabeth stayed in quarters at the palace. Birdie had been to visit a few times for tea, but she had never been dragged in like she was being reprimanded.

"I'm all right," she said.

Elizabeth ushered her into the small cozy room and closed the door.

"I've suspected for some time that things weren't right," she said, looking at Birdie meaningfully. And then her eyes dropped down to Birdie's midsection. It was getting more and more difficult for her to hide. The growing bump on her small frame was starting to get obvious. She had taken to thickening her waistline just slightly with a roll of cotton so that the space between her rib cage and her stomach wasn't quite so pronounced. One looked a bit like weight gain; the other looked purely like pregnancy.

"Everything will be all right," she said.

"Birdie," Elizabeth said. "I'm only going to ask you this once, and I do expect you to be truthful with me. Are you pregnant?"

Birdie stood silent for a long time, then she went and sat in the floral armchair by the fireplace. She picked at the doily that was resting over the forest-green fabric, her heart thundering so hard she could hardly bring herself to speak. But she knew that if she could tell anyone, it was Elizabeth. She was truly frightened now. Because he was looking for another wife, and she hadn't mustered up the courage to speak to him. She didn't know if she ever would. If she ever could.

The pain of him not recognizing her was… It was excruciating. The longer it went on the more it hurt.

That first day she had felt like he'd hit her square in the chest when he'd looked at her and seen nothing. But she'd been so shocked that the full weight of it hadn't fully settled in.

Since then, she'd managed to make herself angry. Devastated. Filled with denial, sometimes. And the time was passing, whether she made a decision about what to do or not.

She was just hiding. Everything. From everyone.

"Yes," she said. "I am."

It was a relief to admit it. Because she'd been keeping it to herself. Hadn't admitted it out loud to anyone. It made it all feel unreal to her. Except her body was changing every day. She felt the symptoms, the exhaustion. And eventually she knew she wasn't going to be able to hide it anymore. She'd always worn her uniform large, to make it easier to move around, and that was about the only thing saving her from exposure now.

Except now she was exposed.

"And your mother?"

"My *stepmother*," she corrected.

"Does she know?"

Birdie shook her head. "That would require the lady to look at me on any given morning before I leave the house, and she rarely ever does that. Not a complaint, I assure you. But I don't think she's aware enough of me to observe anything."

"Good. And the father?"

Birdie clasped her hands in her lap. "I haven't told him."

"Birdie, it looks to me that you are a few months gone."

Birdie nodded. "I am. But I don't know what to do. I don't… He's not someone that I can just speak to."

"Tell me everything," Elizabeth said.

"I… It was the night of the queen's funeral." She looked down at her hands. "I just wanted to comfort him. I just… He's so… He means so much to me and I thought he needed me."

"Birdie," she said, looking so sad and sympathetic it killed Birdie more than if she'd been angry or disapproving. "I know you care very much for the king. I've watched you for years. I know that you adore him. But… He wouldn't… You work in the palace."

"He doesn't know it was me," she said quickly. "It was dark in the room, I knew it was him, because of course I did, because I… I care about him. I've served him for all these years. I thought for sure he must know. But then when I came to serve him the next day he didn't recognize me." A tear slid down her cheeks. "It didn't matter who I was."

"My dear, he didn't force himself on you." Her words were steely and direct.

"No!" Her eyes went wide, and flew to Elizabeth's. "I wanted to do something for him. I wanted to be there for him. I'm the one who caused all of this. And now he… He's looking for a wife. I just overheard him in the office. He was talking to Andrei Ardelean. They're planning on having everyone back, all of the nobles, and he's going to choose a wife at this big masked ball."

Elizabeth looked shocked. "It's only been five months since the queen's death."

"I know. They had that entire discussion. It's all in service of finding someone and delaying the wedding for a year or so. But making sure that it's… What do I do? Do I just tell him? I… I can't bear the rejection. What if he laughs at me? Doesn't believe me. He doesn't have any inkling it was me. I'm in his study every day and I feel alive with it, with the knowledge of what happened between us and he…he barely looks at me."

"My dear," Elizabeth said. "I am so sorry."

"I can't imagine that he's going to be happy when he finds out that he's having a child with me. I'm nothing. I'm no one. It's so ridiculous to him that he would've ever slept with a maid that he looked me full in the face after being inside of me and…" She squeezed her eyes shut. "I'm sorry. I'm saying more than I mean to."

Elizabeth knelt down beside her. "Heartbreak is a terrible thing, my dear, and it's all right for you to acknowledge that you were very intimate with him, and it hurts you that he doesn't see you like you do him. It certainly isn't too much for me to hear."

"Thank you," she said.

"There's only one thing to be done."

"What?"

"He needs to recognize you."

"What? It's a masked ball and I can't go anyway!"

"I have an idea," she said, tapping her chin. "You need to go to the ball."

"But I can't. I won't be invited."

"You weren't invited to the funeral either. You were working. But it's easy, once you're already in the palace, to steal into any room you like. As you well know."

Her cheeks went hot. "I suppose so."

"If he recognizes you, if he sees you and he knows, then he might realize who you are."

"Do you really think so?"

"You could tell him. You can march right up to the office and show him you're pregnant. You could let him see for himself. Or you can make it so he sees you as he did that night."

"And how is that, do you think?"

"You were exactly what he needed, dear girl. If he thinks that that's going to come in the form of an aristocratic woman, then present yourself to him that way. Once he knows, once he sees that you're both, he won't be able to deny you."

"Or," she said, "he'll hate me forever."

"My dear, there are some sad truths about women who bear the issue of kings when they're not married, especially when they're not from the same class. I have deep respect for King Onyx, but he is a king. And a man besides. There is always the risk that he won't acknowledge the child as legitimate. That he may style you as a nanny. Or that he may make you a mistress. That your son will have to exist in the shadows."

Birdie knew that. Deep down she did, and there was no reason for her to believe that it would actually be any different. Because no one in her life treated her like she deserved to be anywhere but in the shadows. That was the truth of it. Her stepmother despised her. Her stepsisters saw her as nothing more than a servant.

They would be doing everything they could to finagle an invitation to the ball, even though they hadn't been at the funeral. Trying to get themselves on the invite list. Trying to get themselves in front of the king. If her stepmother knew that she was having the king's baby she would be outraged.

"You can't hide forever," Elizabeth said. "Or you can. You could leave. You could never speak of it again. You could go and raise your child alone. Not risk yourself."

Birdie shook her head. "No. I'll do it. I'll go to the ball. But I don't… I don't have anything to wear."

Elizabeth smiled. "I have just the thing."

That was how Birdie found herself being ushered out of Elizabeth's quarters, into a wing of the palace that she had rarely ever been in. "You know," Elizabeth said. "I served the queen. Not Queen Circe, Onyx's mother."

She hadn't fully appreciated ever that Elizabeth must have known everyone in the palace for years. That she would've known Onyx when he was a child.

"Oh."

"She has the most glorious wardrobe, still here in the palace. And there's one gown… It would suit you so well, Birdie."

"I can't wear the…the dead queen's dress?"

"What better time? She would have liked you very much. She was such a brave woman. You know, she was common in many ways."

"She was the village leader's daughter," Birdie said. "Of the disenfranchised people that lived in the mountains. Before they unified the country. She was royalty, in her circle."

"Yes. But not in the way the crown had ever acknowledged it before. What she was, was an incredibly brave, strong young woman who took a chance. Even when it was frightening. And she would've seen you, she would've seen how much you cared for her son. I don't wish to speak ill of anyone who has passed. But Onyx's wife didn't… He married for duty."

"The queen was lovely," Birdie said softly.

It was one of the things that had always made her feel so guilty about her crush on the king. Circe had been kind to everyone who worked in the palace. Funny, bold and fashionable, there had been nothing to dislike about her.

"In some ways. She wasn't compatible with the king. At least not to my eyes."

That wasn't something Birdie had seen. She'd thought they were a beautiful couple. So much so that it hurt.

"I have no children of my own," Elizabeth said. "But I have watched Onyx since he was a boy. And I've cared for you since you've come here. I would rather see you on the throne, Birdie, by his side, than any of these noblewomen that might be invited. And you're the one having the heir. No, we can't guarantee that everything will work out. But we must have courage."

She opened up the vast wardrobe, and Birdie walked inside, the array of ball gowns that glittered before her stunning. Elizabeth walked to the back and pulled out a lavender confection of a gown, with lilac netting, and gold vines twining down the bodice. "Oh," she said. "It's beautiful."

"It will do its job covering up your bump."

"Won't he recognize it?"

"I don't think so."

"Try it on."

So she did, and stood before the mirror, barely recognizing herself.

"Leave your hair down," Elizabeth said.

Her hair had been down that night. He pushed his fingers through it. It was wild, far too untamed to let it be down during her workday. But that had been perfect for making love to him.

"All right," she said. "I'll do it."

She truly didn't have a choice.

"The day of the ball, I'll help get you ready. And then I'll position you so that you can enter the ballroom."

"Thank you," she said. "I couldn't have done any of this without you."

"Sometimes a girl just needs a little help," she said. "And a few granted wishes."

Her stomach was tied up in knots. And she wasn't sure if she was going to be able to handle any of this.

But she had to try. She had to have courage.

If he would just recognize her, if he could just know, then maybe all of the feelings that he felt that night would come back up.

And he would feel the same thing that she did.

It was the only hope for her. For him.

And for their baby.

CHAPTER FOUR

If only the lead-up to the ball hadn't been so disastrous.

But the trouble was, invitations were issued to many different families in Basilia, including Birdie's own.

"Does that mean I'm invited?"

It would take a layer of espionage away from her current plan.

"Of course not," her stepmother had said. "It is for my family, my daughters."

"It's for the household," Birdie said.

"They won't be needing you at the palace that day," her stepmother said.

"Well, I don't know if they will."

"You must try to get it off. We're going to need help getting ready. It's going to take a team, and we can't afford a team."

"This is ridiculous," Birdie said. "They're not going to meet the king."

"Birdie," her stepmother said. "Even if this isn't going to get one of them on the throne, that room is going to be filled with rich men. Your stepsisters marrying one of those men will benefit you."

How? Birdie wasn't even part of the household enough to be included in this invitation in the eyes of her stepmother. She had stayed, and she had helped take care of them because it had been her father's dying request. That she not leave them alone. But her stepmother was just so cold and so dismissive. The hints of outright cruelty Birdie sometimes saw in her chilled her to the bone.

She didn't want to show any difference in her behavior. But she was beginning to plan. Beginning to try to imagine a life where she wasn't so under her stepmother's thumb. Of course, the real issue was that she had agreed a long time ago to let her paycheck go into a family account, and then on top of that she would have to find a new place to stay, which on her income would be difficult.

Extricating herself without letting her stepmother know would be difficult. The axe would have to fall all at once, and she was wondering if it even mattered. Because if she succeeded with what she wanted to do the night of the ball…

Still, she did what her stepmother asked and got the night off.

"What are you doing?" Elizabeth asked.

"You'll help me, right? I can't afford for my stepmother to get wind of anything. She has an invitation to this ball, and she will make my life difficult. If she has any suspicions…"

The older woman hesitated, her expression pained. Birdie understood she was asking for a lot. That all of this was irregular and putting Elizabeth at risk, potentially, and she hated to ask that. Wouldn't if it didn't feel so, so important.

"I understand," Elizabeth said.

Birdie nodded, swallowing as best she could through her tightened throat. "I have to get out from under her thumb. But it's just not that easy."

"You can always stay with me," Elizabeth said.

Birdie knew that. Losing her mother had been a terrible blow, and nothing would ever replace her. But where her stepmother had never offered her anything, Elizabeth had stepped in and become such a wonderful, soft, caring force in her life.

"Elizabeth, one way or the other, everything is going to break open. I can't hide the pregnancy forever. I'll either be staying with you, living in the shadows like you said that I might because the king doesn't want to acknowledge the baby publicly or… This is my one hope."

"I'll give you everything to take to your house so that you can get ready there. I'll make sure that you get led into the palace. It won't be impossible. It's just more difficult."

"I know. There was no other way."

"I know, Birdie." Elizabeth stepped forward and put her hand on Birdie's cheek, before tucking her hair behind her ear. "It's very difficult to try and soar when so many people have tried to clip your wings. But you are very brave."

"And maybe very foolish," she said.

Elizabeth smiled, sad and wistful. "Maybe. But love makes fools of all of us. I was in love once."

"You were?"

She looked down. "Yes. And if there's one regret I have in my life it's that I didn't work harder for that love. It requires bravery to love. To try and demolish the barriers surrounding it. You are doing that. It's extremely brave. And in the end, worth it. Because to live a life without doubt and regret must be a beautiful thing."

Birdie's throat tightened. "I hope so."

She stashed the gown in her attic room, and worked on the mask in the evenings. A basic, cheap shape that she'd ordered online, and was hand beading to match the vines on her dress.

Once everyone in the house left, she would be able to get herself ready and go to the ball. She would be a little bit late, but it wouldn't be the end of the world. She would've had to be late even if she'd been at the palace. Because she was going to have to finagle her way past anyone checking a guest list no matter where her starting point was.

She was no Cinderella, and there were no enchanted mice and pumpkins to help usher her in, so she had to be clever if she couldn't be magic.

With her plan firmly in place, she was feeling better about the night. Even though she was sick with nerves. It was getting harder and harder to hide her condition as the weeks ticked by, and she was starting to get worried she was going to have to let the dress out for the ball. When it came to uniforms, it was simple. As easy as making a trade in the laundry facility. New uniforms were always available for staff for free.

A bespoke, valuable gown was another matter. But thank God, the day of the ball arrived, and she could still zip herself into it. She'd never had such cleavage in her life.

Which ordinarily she might be pleased about, because she did look very good in the dress, but she needed the king to recognize her on instinct. And if there was one thing he did know intimately it was her body.

Does he? Or is this all wishful thinking? Is this all foolishness?

Maybe he was only thinking of the queen. Maybe he was only thinking of his own needs.

Maybe he didn't really want you at all.

She took the gown off, and stuck it in the back of her closet, and then went downstairs to begin helping her sisters get ready.

"I wonder if we can film a dance at the palace," Alana said, looking at her reflection in the mirror. Her stepsister's breasts were taped into her dress, her cleavage a truly impressive feat. She hated that it made her feel insecure. That both of her stepsisters were beautiful, in spite of the fact that they were ridiculous.

Natalie had strands of pink curls woven through her hair, and genuinely, it should've looked stupid. But she seemed vivacious and pretty, and maybe the king would like that.

No. What a nightmare. She could not deal with a future where Onyx married either of them, and what she knew about him didn't seem to indicate that he would ever be interested in anyone like them.

Finally, they were ready, and she began to head back to her own room, when her stepmother met her at the center of the stairs. "What is this?"

She was holding the mask that Birdie had spent all that time on in her hands.

"It's nothing," she said, her stomach tight.

"Were you planning on trying to go to the ball?"

"No. I'm not invited. They won't let me in."

"Why do you have a gown in your closet?"

"It's nothing. It was a gift from someone at work, and of course I took it because why wouldn't you take a gift that pretty?"

"It's too much of a coincidence," she said.

She grabbed Birdie's arm and started to drag her up the stairs. Birdie wrapped her arm around her stomach protectively, concern for her precarious position on the stairs and her baby the only thing keeping her from fighting her stepmother, even though the other woman was much taller than she was.

She found herself shoved into the room. "This is why I wanted you here. I don't trust you. The look on your face every time the king is mentioned…" Suddenly, her eyes went down to Birdie's stomach.

"You little slut."

"I… Nothing to do with—"

She snapped the mask in half and threw it at Birdie. "I'll deal with you later. We have to go."

She swept out of the room, and Birdie heard the lock click. Panic overtook her.

She was trapped.

Locked in the room. And there was nothing she could do. She wasn't going to be able to go to the ball. Her mask was broken. She fought the urge to lie on the ground and curl into a ball, to sob like a motherless child. Because that's what she was. She had never given in to that particular despair. She'd never felt so lost, so alone. She'd always been overcome by the drive to keep going. To keep hoping.

But not now.

Now she felt like she was lost. Utterly and totally lost.

Then she looked to the side and saw her phone.

She wasn't alone.

She might be alone in this room but she wasn't alone in the world, and she wouldn't give up. Not now. Maybe she didn't have enchanted mice or fairy godmothers, but she had Elizabeth.

She had hope after all.

She was sobbing, great gasping breaths. Her stepmother would know it was her when she arrived at the palace. She would *know*. But she had to try. She had to.

With shaking hands she called Elizabeth. "Elizabeth," she said. "My stepmother locked me in my room. She found out she... I don't know what to do."

"Don't worry," she said. "I'll send you help."

"My mask is ruined..."

"Don't worry," Elizabeth reiterated. "I'm sending someone to help you."

She didn't know who that would be, or what was going to happen. But with as much faith as she could muster she got dressed, unpinned her hair and let it loose. And when she heard the lock being rattled outside the door, she stood. Two of the palace drivers appeared in the room.

"Elizabeth said you were in trouble." The first to speak was Adam, a man she'd known at the palace for years. In his fifties, and handsome, with salt-and-pepper hair. There was a kindness about him that had always made Birdie feel fond of him, but this was beyond anything she'd expected from anyone ever.

"I... Thank you."

"Not to worry," the other one said, younger and boyish, new enough she didn't know his name. He handed her a delicate mesh mask. "She also said that you need to get to the ball."

"I do," she said.

"She has these for you also," Adam said. He held up a pair of shoes, delicate and glimmering, translucent. "She said you needed shoes that were suitable to the dress."

"Oh," she said. "They're beautiful."

She'd never been so close to total despair as she was a few moments ago, and now it felt like everything was…okay. Almost.

She was going to have to make it into the ballroom and connect with the king as quickly as possible. "We have to get you to the ball," Adam said.

Suspicion stirred in her chest. He'd always been kind, but this was so above and beyond, it was potentially risking his job if they were caught sneaking her in. "Why are you doing this?"

"I would do anything for Elizabeth," he said.

Birdie wrapped her arms around his neck, hugging him. "She would do anything for you," she whispered, just so he could hear. "I'm certain of it. However you feel, you need to tell her."

He didn't say anything, but as she was whisked down the stairs and into a beautiful, classic town car, she felt like this was a night when anything was possible.

All of her wishes had been answered.

Everything would be okay.

CHAPTER FIVE

FAR TOO QUICKLY, the masked ball was upon them. He both wanted it to happen, and didn't. He disliked parties generally. And would never have agreed to do this if he didn't think it was the absolute best option to find the woman.

She haunted him.

He'd never in his life had sex like that.

Maybe it was an illusion. Maybe it was all intensity brought on by the moment. By the loss.

It was such a difficult, conflicting thing to miss Circe the way that he did. He hadn't loved her. Their marriage had been difficult. But she'd been a presence in his life. A woman who'd had fire and strength. And who certainly had deserved to live. To go on with her life, to be a mother, to have the things that she wanted.

He felt… That he hadn't been able to make her happy was something that ate at him more and more as time went on. That her life, the past few years of it were spent in a state of dissatisfaction. Should he have set her free, let her go off and find someone else that she could love? They'd both been so wedded to their duty. Far more than they were wedded to each other.

And yet the end result had been the same. She had

been a captive in her own life, and that was how it had been until the end.

He was looking into bringing another woman into this. Into *him*.

But at least there was spark. He clung to that. He'd been so convinced that he and Circe would be able to create a spark out of a shared belief in what needed to happen for the kingdom.

But they hadn't.

And if they had at least been able to be companionable then perhaps it would've been acceptable, but they hadn't even been friends.

They'd been two strangers, bristling with resentment and loneliness.

And he missed her. Because he didn't know how to live without that. Didn't know how to be by himself, even when the togetherness had been difficult.

To believe that he might be on the cusp of something else was…impossible.

"Are you all right?"

He looked at his sister, who was staring at him with large, concerned eyes, her son on her hip, his pudgy hand clasping the neckline of her green ball gown. She was going to leave him in the nursery before everything got started, he assumed. Knowing Emerald, she might decide to bring the baby for a while. Being able to have a family, a happy, intact family, was such a great joy for her that she often brought her child when no other princess would ever consider such a thing.

He didn't blame her. He was such a joy for the three of them, who had experienced so much loss.

Circe had loved him too.

"Fine," he said.

His sister knew why he was having the ball. That was another issue with having your best friend be married to your sister. Andrei was going to report back. Even if Onyx didn't particularly want Emerald to know the details of his intimate life.

But Emerald hadn't been judgmental; she'd been desperate to help take up the charge and plan everything. She was incredibly critical of Circe, and of their relationship, which only made him feel defensive of his late wife. He'd told her as much, but she'd said that all she really wanted was for him to be happy. Was for him to find what he needed, and to have the kind of love that she and Andrei had.

He wasn't sure that was possible for him. He was a man whose life was marked by duty. But he would take some passion. He'd tasted it, if only for a fleeting moment. If he could just have that...

"You don't seem fine."

"I am. I'm going to discover if she was an apparition or a real woman, I suppose."

The suspense of that was more than he could bear. He just needed it to start.

It was a strange thing to want something for himself. He had wanted only what was good for the nation for a very long time.

But living in the mess made by his previous marriage had showed him that there was a real cost to that.

The real cost had been Circe's happiness. The entire last part of her life spent in misery with him.

Emerald put her hand on his shoulder. "You deserve to find love," she said.

"Thank you," he said. Because there really was no point in telling her love wasn't the ultimate goal. In telling her he wasn't entirely sure what drove him other than desire. He'd never been in a position where he could explore that. Maybe this was just the kind of insanity he might've experienced when he was a teenage boy. Maybe he wasn't being driven by anything lofty now. Maybe he was lying to himself. Telling himself that he was doing this in response to Circe's unhappiness.

Maybe he was only doing it for his libido.

He would hardly be the first man to do so.

As was customary, he allowed the ball to start, making his entrance ten minutes after. He scanned the room. He didn't see her. Which was a ridiculous thing, because he'd never seen her in a great amount of detail. She'd been nothing more than an impression. She'd been…a feeling. And he was counting on that feeling to guide him now.

It was one reason he appreciated the concept of the masked ball. It was the best way to recapture that moment. Reclaim that connection.

Be driven by *feeling*.

By that moment he'd been wrapped up in with her. It had nothing to do with who he was, or who she was. It had everything to do with a kind of magical enchantment, a spell that had come over him. He wanted to feel that again.

He needed to feel it again.

He moved around the room, looking at all of the gorgeous women in their dresses, and they were gorgeous. Confections of fuchsia, bright blue and electric green. Elaborate masks, and beautiful hairstyles. If she felt the same thing he did, she would be here.

He thought of the way her curls had felt sliding through his fingers. She had been so delicate. No one here was quite that.

He could remember how she smelled. The scent of her skin. The lilacs.

He was looking for that now. She wasn't here.

"Your Highness."

It was rare for anyone to approach him in the ballroom. Typical protocol demanded he make the first move in any social interaction, and he was taken aback by the tall, redheaded woman in a garish orange gown, clutching two fluttering young women to her side.

"I'm Lady Tremaine. My husband was a very well known businessman in the country before his untimely death, and I was so sorry to hear about your wife, because of course I understand your grief."

He could see this clearly for what it was and clinging to his manners now was a feat more challenging than it had ever been.

"These are my daughters. Alana and Natalie and—"

And then, there was a rustle in the room, and he turned to look the same direction as everyone else. Arriving down the stairs, her hair a glorious blond halo, all dressed in lilac, the mask that covered her face a glimmering silver and gold with vines. She was like a fairy. And he *knew*.

As much as he could know anything.

With each step she took down the stairs, her shoes glimmered and glistened, her dress a pastel aura around her. Such a contrast with all of the brightness.

"What is she doing here?" The question was asked

with venom, the woman who'd just spoken so sweetly to him now looking murderous.

Was it as obvious to her as it was to everyone? That this woman was magic. Singular.

He took a step toward the stairs and the woman reached out and took his arm. "Your Highness, that is no one. She's… That woman is…"

"You will take your hands off of me, Lady Tremaine," he said, knowing full well his glare had the power to turn even the bravest man's blood to ice. "And you will not speak ill about her."

He began to walk toward the stairs, hearing a ripple in the room as he did.

And then her eyes met his.

She stopped, and he kept moving toward her.

He went up two steps to meet her. "You're here," he said.

She nodded, not speaking, her eyes darting behind him for a moment. He could see worry on her face, in her gaze.

Maybe this had haunted her as it had haunted him.

And he extended his hand. "My lady," he said. "Will you dance with me?"

She nodded slowly, and he took her hand, the instant, electric need that shot through him unlike anything he'd ever experienced before.

Except that night. Except when she had touched his face. And everything had changed. He pulled her close to him, and he smelled her. Lilacs.

And then, he swirled her out onto the dance floor, in front of everyone. She was here. She had come.

She smiled up at him, and he felt like the world had shifted somehow. Like everything was different.

All of it changing in a moment.

He never felt like this. He hadn't been sure that he was capable of it. When he had thought about it at all. His own feelings had never mattered. Not until her.

There was a squeezing guilt that went along with that. It'd taken the death of someone else for him to ever experience something like magic.

But he pushed that aside, because there was no reason to think about it now. She was here. In his arms. It didn't matter what her name was. It didn't matter who she was. Nothing mattered but how much he wanted her.

But they were dancing in a room full of people, and he had to keep his desire on a leash. He couldn't betray that he already knew her. The cost was far too high. Andrei was right. There was a way to play this, one that would honor the crown, honor Circe's memory.

He couldn't take her. Not tonight. And certainly not in front of everyone. Except…

Just for a moment. He could steal her away just for a moment. The guests already had eyes on them. He had already made a spectacle. Perhaps everyone could feel this thing that was arcing between them.

"Will you step outside with me?"

She nodded, but didn't say a word. He hungered for her voice. The husky whisper from that night.

With her hand in his, he led her out the back doors of the ballroom. There were many people out on the terrace, and they slipped through the knot of the crowd easily, heading down the stairs and toward the garden.

"I need…" He grabbed her, tugged her behind a

hedge, like he was a green boy, and pulled her into his arms. He kissed her like he was starving, because he was. Because there had never been anything before her like this, and he feared that there would be nothing after. Because she was singular, and his need for her was something like he had never imagined possible.

She wrapped her arms around his neck, her body arching forward. He cupped the back of her head, and kissed her. Deep and long. "You came," he said.

"Of course," she whispered. "I had to… I had to see you."

There would be time for talking later. He needed to know her. Everything about her. All of his good intentions, the idea of taking this slow. *I'm not claiming her tonight…* All of his thoughts melted away. Because he needed her. He moved his hand down to cup her breast. It felt fuller than when they had been together last. Or maybe it was just that she was better than any dream he'd ever had.

Maybe it was just that it had been so good his own imagination had blunted it, because not even he could believe it. Even having experienced it. He moved his hand down to her waist, and then around to her stomach.

Her rounded stomach.

He had taken her without a condom. That night, he had taken her without a condom. He had known that, but somewhere in the back of his mind he had assumed that if a woman had come to him, if she'd slept with him without any mention of birth control, that she was protected.

He ended the kiss, his hand planted firmly on her stomach. "Are you…?"

"I… Yes," she said.

"Why didn't you tell me before this? You knew where to find me. I had no idea where to find you."

"I didn't know what to do," she whispered. "But… perhaps…it's a good thing?"

She was so hopeful. But nothing about this was good. Her pregnancy would announce to the world that he had taken another woman the night he had buried his wife. The disrespect on Circe's legacy, on his own, was unfathomable. And of course that wasn't her fault, unless…

He didn't know who she was.

She had come to him, they had spoken no words, they hadn't used protection and she hadn't protested. All this had been a plot. To get herself pregnant with the heir. Or perhaps to pass her pregnancy off as his.

The look on Lady Tremaine's face when she'd come in…

"Who are you?" he asked.

He grabbed the edge of her mask and took it away from her face, revealing herself to him.

Yes, it was the woman from that night. But it was…

The moonlight illuminated her more than the harsh firelight of the study. And suddenly, those features looked familiar. Much more than they had that night, and yet, he questioned how he hadn't seen it.

Of course.

She wasn't noble. She wasn't a princess, a duchess, anything.

It was the maid.

And she had contrived to carry the heir, she had overheard about the ball…

It might not even be his child. She might just be trying to pass it off as his. That would make perfect sense.

If she had fallen pregnant by some no-account man, and had decided to take an opportunity to use his grief against him. Coming to him under cover of darkness, touching him when he was vulnerable…

"*You*," he said, the word filled with all the poison now flooding his veins. "How dare you?"

"Your Highness," she said. "I can explain. I…"

He couldn't bear to hear her speak. Couldn't bear to hear her lies, not now.

"You will be explaining. At length. But away from here. You will not go back to the ball, you will go to my study. I know you know where it is."

Her eyes were round and glimmering, like she was innocent, like she was the victim. "Are you angry with me?"

"*Angry* doesn't begin to cover it," he ground out. "*Angry* isn't strong enough."

He would tear down the whole sky and leave them standing in the shattered stars. He would bring down the moon. He would…

He would blot out the night, the day, everything, right the wrong that had been done here.

A maid. A commoner.

Another trap.

"But I don't understand. You want me. You want this." As if she were so confused about why he would be angry. About the abuse she'd committed here.

"I would *never* have wanted you if I would've known who you were," he said. "And you must have known that. Otherwise, you would've revealed yourself. Otherwise, you would've revealed your pregnancy."

She clasped her hands in front of her, still trying to

play the innocent. "I came into the study the next day and you clearly didn't know. I thought you did. I—"

"Liar. Go to my office. I must finish here, and then I will go and find you."

She shook her head. Gathered the dress in her arms, and moved away from him. "No."

He took a step toward her, rage driving him. "You dare to defy me?"

It was her turn to hold her ground, that innocence transforming then to outrage. "I'm not going to subject myself to more of your scorn. I've had enough of it. For the whole rest of my life. I've taken it from my family for years, I'll be damned if I take it from you. If I ever expose my child to such a thing."

She pulled away from him, stepping back and tripping in the grass, before kicking her shoes off. Then she turned and ran from him. Leaving him shocked. He moved slowly over to where she had discarded the first shoe, bending down and picking it up, holding it in his hand.

He heard movement behind him, and he turned. Andrei was there.

"How much of that did you hear?"

"I only heard a yell, and came over." He looked down and saw the shoe in Onyx's hand. "I take it that didn't go well."

"I need you to send your guards to her house."

"Who? The woman that you…"

"Yes."

"Who is she?"

He looked grimly at the empty expanse of darkness that she'd vanished into. "The maid."

CHAPTER SIX

SHE COULDN'T GO back to the palace. She knew that. She was in abject misery, and she knew that the only reason her stepmother hadn't thrown her out into the street was that she was trying to play all of this to the best of her advantage.

She was pregnant with Onyx's child, and even though her stepmother hadn't told her stepsisters, she knew that she was weighing how to use it. That she had realized it. Even without the two of them speaking of it. When she had arrived home that night after the dreadful encounter with Onyx, where he had accused her of all manner of unfair and unimaginable things, when he had turned not into the cherished lover or beloved king that she had known before, but into a monster, her stepmother had met her at the door.

"I take it that didn't go to plan."

"No," she said, looking her stepmother full in the face because she had no intention of being cowed. She could not be more humiliated than she already was. She couldn't even face Elizabeth. Even though the other woman had known there was a possibility this could happen, even though Birdie had known, it was the vitriol in his voice, in his face, that had truly wounded her.

It was unconscionable to him that she was the mother of his child. That she was the one he'd slept with.

"Poor Birdie. At least you'll always have your family."

It had been a threat, not a comfort, and Birdie was simply waiting for exactly what might happen.

Would her stepmother sell her story to the press? Would she attempt to blackmail the palace? Any of those things were possible for her stepmother, also secret, maniacal options that Birdie—as a normal human being—couldn't fathom.

And so she had been waiting. Until the day the king arrived at her house.

"Go upstairs," her stepmother said.

"Absolutely not," Birdie said. "I have to speak to him."

If he was here, then it meant maybe they could have a reasonable conversation. Maybe. Even if they couldn't quite rise to the level of reasonable, as she had been sitting with all of this for the past few days, she knew that she did need to see him again. Because they had to come to an agreement about how they were going to handle this. Even though she was bitter at him, hated him almost as much as she'd ever loved him for the way that he had hurt her that night, she knew that they had to have a conversation.

He was a king, and she had very little power.

She also had no money to take care of her child. Her child's father was a king, and that child was owed his father's money. Status. It had nothing to do with what Birdie wanted for herself. Everything to do with the fact that as it was in her power, she would make her child comfortable.

Undoubtedly, the king would see that as evidence that she was a gold digger. She didn't care. Her own father had left her with nothing to her name. Her stepmother had control of absolutely everything—such as it was. It had left Birdie vulnerable to this abuse by her family, and one thing she would never, ever do was leave her child vulnerable. Nor would she allow a father to dodge his financial responsibility. To put anything before that child.

She loved her father. It was difficult for her to admit to herself that he had let her down. Easier to blame her stepmother, who was still here, and actively causing harm in her life. But the truth was, her father could have protected her. He should have known his wife well enough to have seen that she would give everything to herself, and her own children, that she would never treat Birdie like one of her own.

He hadn't done that for her. Whether because he was blinded by his love, or because he didn't want to make waves. Birdie refused to be blinded, and she would make waves. She would make a whole typhoon if she had to.

"I said get upstairs."

"And I said no."

"You ungrateful little brat."

"What do I have to be grateful for? You've done nothing but abuse me, treat me like a servant. You've done nothing but spend the money that I earn and—"

She grabbed the back of Birdie's neck, and pinned

her arm behind her back, forcing her to begin marching up the stairs. "Stop," Birdie shouted.

"You will get upstairs. Or I will throw you down them. And then what will happen to your royal meal ticket?"

Stunned by the cruelty, Birdie didn't fight as she was shoved into the attic room, the door locked firmly behind her.

She could hear her stepmother going back downstairs and she pressed her ear to the door, trying to hear what was going on. She closed her eyes, her heart throbbing in her chest.

It was the strangest thing to be suspended in this moment. Where both the king and her stepmother felt like her adversaries, and she had to root for one of them.

No. You don't. You root for yourself. Yes. She was on her own team. Her own side. She cared about her future. And the future of her child. If Onyx couldn't be the man that she had dreamed he was, she would be everything that her child needed. She would be the mother that she had always longed to know. She would be everything her child needed, but it started now. It started with facing them both down. She had never considered herself downtrodden. But over the years, her world had gotten smaller and smaller, and things that should've felt outrageous had begun to feel reasonable. The way that her stepmother treated her. The way that she locked her away. The way that she had been so controlled. The way her entire life was situated around other people. Their desires. Their comfort. She had thought that it was acceptable because they were family. Because it was the last thing her father had said to her. And then, she had begun to idolize Onyx.

Because he was beautiful. Because she saw him every day and he treated her with the most basic kindness. But when she had needed him most he had betrayed her. And so now she had clarity.

She would fly with her own wings.

She wouldn't wait for anyone's permission; she wouldn't wait for their acceptance or their kindness.

She had courage. That was all that mattered.

She went into the bathroom and began to dig through her makeup bag. Inside, she found all of the pins that she used to secure her hair every day for her work at the palace. She smiled just slightly, because they would be her route to freedom. She began to fiddle with the lock in the door, bending and twisting and contorting one hairpin, bringing down one of the lock mechanisms, and letting that pin rest there as she grabbed another and twisted it, driving it through the center of the lock until she heard it click.

And then, Birdie freed herself.

She stepped right out of the attic, lifted her chin high and began to walk down the stairs. She heard voices, angry male voices, and the sound of her stepmother, who was also angry, but clearly continuing to try to insert herself into this whole situation with the king.

"She has run away, Your Highness. She is such a treasonous and willful girl. I wouldn't be surprised if she was trying to pass the child of another man off as yours. She isn't faithful. It's one reason I've had to keep such an eye on her all these years. It's done her well to work at the palace because it keeps her focused. Without which I fear she runs about spreading her legs for everyone and everything."

Just then, Birdie reached the bottom of the stairs, and rounded the corner to the entryway.

"Isn't it so nice that I was able to take a break from my whoring to attend to this conversation that seems to be about me."

Her stepmother whirled around. "What are you doing here?"

"Did you not remember that you locked me in the attic? A couple of hairpins sorted me out just fine."

"Locked in the attic?"

For the first time, she forced herself to look at Onyx. He was flanked by Andrei, the two of them looking like angels of death. Onyx held one of her shoes in his hand.

"I have come to retrieve you," he said.

"I don't recall asking to be retrieved."

"It is a command. From your king."

"Your Highness, with no offense meant whatsoever, you had your opportunity for me to go with you willingly. You spoiled it."

"But I am a king, and so my word will be law, will it not?"

She realized then, that while she didn't wish to go with him forever, that while she didn't wish to rely on him, she might need to use him as a getaway car. She was hardly going to break past him and his head of security. That was a bit ambitious, even for her. Even for the maternal surge of determination and protectiveness that had risen up in her breast.

"All right. I will go with you. But whether or not I stay with you is another matter."

His dark eyes flashed with rage. "I don't think you understand what's happening here. I am the king. You are in no position to make demands. You are—"

"I know," she said. "I'm a servant. I mean nothing to you. I am little more than an inconvenience to be dealt with to you. But to me, I am a woman. Entirely. With my own hopes and my own dreams, with my own goals."

Conviction built within her breast as she spoke, as she found it in her to not only say the words, but to believe them. As she found her own strength, not in promises she made to her father, not in the feelings she'd been carrying for Onyx, but in her own spine of steel, her own desires.

"And nothing, not my stepmother, and not a king, will keep me from being the mother that I want to be. Both of you are so busy spinning narratives about how you think I might be, and I am here." She turned to her stepmother. "All I ever wanted was for you to be a mother. And when I saw that that wouldn't ever happen, I wanted you to at least show me kindness. But you couldn't even do that. I'm no threat to you. I've done everything that you've ever asked me to do. And still, you will not allow me to be part of this family. And you." She turned to the king. "I cared for you. I saw something in you. Kindness. And I'm a fool for that, because when I needed your kindness it wasn't there. I don't believe it ever was. Which means, I was mistaken. The both of you have left me feeling ill used. But between the two, I will choose you, Your Highness. Because if there's one thing I know how to do, it is defer to the one in power for as long as I must. And that's all it is." She looked at her stepmother. "It's all it is. There is no loyalty left within me, and if I should ever gain any power in this country, I will bestow nothing good upon you."

Onyx grabbed her arm, and looked at her, his gaze full of fury. "I would not count on power."

"Then let's get the rest of the humiliation going, shall we?"

He pulled her out the front door, and her stepmother seemed to animate, shouting as they went. "I will alert the media that you have kidnapped my stepdaughter."

"You will receive a payment. Keep your mouth quiet."

And that was all it took to quiet her stepmother.

Birdie wished emphatically that the woman would get nothing. No money of any kind. But he seemed determined to silence her. That money would be the fastest way to do it.

There were two cars outside. One, a black town car, and the other a limousine. Andrei got into the town car, while Onyx pushed her into the back of the limo, and followed behind.

Once the door was closed behind them, the car was nothing but silent. "Is what your stepmother said true?"

"Now you ask me?"

"Yes," he said. "I'm asking you."

"How nice for me. Finally, I'm being consulted on myself."

"I do not have time for you to have an attitude."

"Yes. I am actually the Whore of Babylon that was foretold in the Book of Revelation. Sorry to disappoint you. The child might actually be the Antichrist."

His expression was shocked. Surely no one had ever spoken to him like this before, but then, he'd probably never put anyone in this position before. She had nothing left to lose. Not her pride, not a single thing. She might as well let him have it. Utterly.

"I've never known you to be sharp-tongued in all the time you've worked in my study," he said.

She laughed. "Because you don't know me. Because I was a fixture. An appliance. A figment of your imagination. I have only ever been what is convenient for me to be in your mind. An invisible waif who brings you tea. A fantasy woman who gives you pleasure. A beautiful aristocrat for you to seduce in the garden, and once I became myself in that moment, it was easier for you to make me into a villain." She paused to try to collect herself. "Do you think that you know your servants, Your Highness? Do you think that we show you the substance of who we are? I meant what I said. What I am very, very good at is being the thing that is required of me. But I have reached my end with that. I am going to be a mother. And I cannot care about your feelings regarding being a father to a child being carried by a commoner. Your feelings don't concern me. If you would like to let me out of this car now, I'll go. I won't ask for a thing from you. I will make my own way, because that is something that I am very good at. Surviving. I will survive. And I'll do it without you."

"Is the child mine?"

"It is a ridiculous thing that you must continue to reframe a question you already have the answer to. I have not introduced this distrust. You have."

"You maintain that it's mine?" he pressed.

"Do a paternity test. I'm not engaging in debates about the state of my uterus with you."

Silence fell in the car.

"You are contentious," he said.

"No, Your Highness. I'm not allowing you to speak and let your insults go unanswered. I think you will find that you are the contentious one."

She was proud of herself for that. If there was one thing she would do, it was stand on business for herself. For her child.

He picked up his phone, and made a call. "I must arrange for a paternity test to be done at the palace. In utero… Yes… Thank you."

He hung the phone up and she simply sat there, looking straight ahead, refusing to meet his eye.

For all that she felt powered by her anger now, she also felt so sorry for herself. And pity wasn't usually an emotion that she let herself feel. But this could've been different. And it was a mystery to her why nobody in her life treated her like she mattered, treated her like she could be trusted. There was nothing she could do about it. She couldn't make people care about her. She couldn't make…

He wasn't different. He was the same. It was a short drive to the palace, and one she knew well. But she didn't typically get delivered right to the front doors, and she was never ushered through them. She went through the servants' entrance. And as they went through those doors, she was stunned when they were rushed by Elizabeth, and by Princess Emerald.

"Onyx, what are you doing?"

"Your Highness, I beg of you."

Onyx stopped, and looked at both his servant and his sister. "This is none of either of your business." His gaze landed on Elizabeth especially hard. "You are speaking out of turn."

"I've known you since you were a child," she said. "And I believed a certain thing about you. About your honor. You have disgraced it with Birdie. She is a lovely girl. And I've watched over her since she first came to the palace, as I watched over you. I'm not speaking out of turn. I'm speaking as someone who watched you grow into the man you are. And I'm uncertain how you became this version of yourself."

"You are dismissed," Onyx said.

Elizabeth held his gaze, then turned on her heel and walked away, leaving Birdie standing there, her heart pounding. "She cares for me," Birdie said. "I don't want her to face any consequences for—"

"You are in no position to negotiate."

"But I am," Emerald said, moving to Birdie's side. She never had much interaction with Princess Emerald, and was surprised that she was taking up her cause now. "What exactly are you doing?"

"This is something I have to figure out myself," Onyx said.

"You're unraveling," Emerald said. "Storming some woman's house and dragging her back here? She's not a prisoner."

"For all intents and purposes at the moment, she is. And when I need your input, I'll ask for it."

"I am furious at you," Emerald said.

"I'll survive," Onyx responded.

And with that, swept Birdie through the entry, and up the stairs toward his study. It didn't take long for clinicians to arrive after that. There was an explanation of

how the fetal DNA would be collected, and Birdie felt
a rush of anxiety as she was prepped for the procedure.

She had agreed to this. In fact, it had been her idea.
Because she wasn't going to argue with him. She wasn't
going to justify herself. She certainly wasn't going to
admit that she had been a trembling virgin when he had
taken her. Because it said too much about her own feelings for him, and while she hadn't been embarrassed
about them before, she was now. Because he had taken
something lovely and turned it into something vile. She
didn't care for it in the least.

Once the procedure was done, neither of them spoke.

"It will take a few hours to process the results."

"As soon as they're ready, let me know."

And then they were left there, just the two of them,
in the study where she normally served him.

"There is nothing to do but wait," he said. "You will
be shown to your bedroom."

"What's the point of giving me a bedroom? Why
don't you just throw me in the dungeon?"

"It's a possibility."

"Do you know what I'm looking forward to?" she
asked. "It's you finding out the results of the test. Because I already know what they are. And here is a fun
bit of information for you. What you're going to discover is that I didn't do anything to you. You have fashioned me into an adversary because you find the truth
of what you did to be inconvenient. You're the villain.
I'm not. I was a servant who walked into your library
after your wife's funeral. I offered you comfort. You
wanted sex. I gave it to you. I'm a servant, and you're a
king, could I have denied you? I made no move to hide

my identity. You simply didn't recognize me. And now you're treating me like I set out to trick you. This is a betrayal of your own making. But yes. I'm happy to be shown to my room now."

He waved a hand, and then went and opened up his study door. "Will you please show the lady to her quarters."

Andrei was standing outside looking stone-faced. And he led her out of the study, up the stairs, and she said nothing as he held the door open for her, and ushered her into a lushly appointed bedroom. "I hope your wife doesn't make you sleep on the couch tonight," Birdie said.

Andrei lifted a brow. "You have quite the attitude."

"It's called matching energy," she said. And with that, he left her there. Then on shaking legs, she walked over to the bed.

Then she threw herself down on it, and cried until she couldn't breathe.

CHAPTER SEVEN

Onyx sat in his study, a glass of whiskey in his hand. His sister hadn't allowed him to dismiss her quite so easily, and that was, yet again, an issue with having his brother-in-law as his chief of security; there was no keeping her out. Because Andrei was never going to side with Onyx. Not on matters that included Emerald. Onyx was already sitting there, awash in a strange sort of shame.

Because he hadn't known that the woman who had come to him that night was a servant. And he had immediately gone to the power that a person with bad intent could hold to ruin his reputation. But what she had spoken of was the disparity in their actual power.

Had she wanted to have sex with him? She said that she had.

But when she put it that way, it was… It was grim, was what it was.

He held power over her, not just as the king of the nation, but direct power to end her job.

Had she been forced to say yes to him? Had that entire night been something that he viewed through the wrong lens? And then he had… Well, he had been awful to her. Emerald was there in his office, looking at him like he was as low as he felt like he might be.

"I have never known you to treat a woman this way."

"You have never known that part of me," he said.

In truth, he had never known this part of himself. This was sharp and jagged, with no control to be found at all. A disaster, in short.

He'd been so careful with his assignations when he was younger, and then he had been married. This was him, and the consequences of passion. It was something he'd never navigated before. Something he had no experience with.

And apparently, he didn't react well to it.

"What if she is pregnant with your child?"

He hadn't been worried about that. He had been solely focused on his anger. He had been convinced there was no way that it could be his child, and he had only convinced himself further in the days since the ball.

Now he was actually grappling with it. In these hours before the test results came in.

What if she was? Well, then there was no question; he would have to marry her. He was not the sort of man who would keep a mistress. And he was definitely not the sort of man who would keep a child in the shadows. Who would make a bastard out of an heir. And he needed an heir. So there was no point to it besides. But it would lay bare his own failings. There would be no covering this up. The entirety of the kingdom—the world—would be able to do the math on this. There was no rescuing the optics.

And there was quite possibly no rescuing the relationship that he had now begun with Birdie.

Birdie. Roberta. A commoner, who may very well end up being his next queen. A woman who would hate him just as much as his first wife.

And it was his fault. Perhaps all of it was his fault.

He had handled this in all the wrong ways, but he had no idea what else he might've done.

Not been a raging dick?

Well. There was that. But everything felt so…precarious. He was afraid to hope that it was his child, and he was also afraid that it might be.

"You could've handled it differently."

"Really? Thank you. I appreciate you jumping in in the eleventh hour to lecture me."

"It isn't a lecture. It's a truth. You could've been better."

"I'm sorry to disappoint you. But I am not… No matter how much I might try, I am not a figurehead. And I'm not someone that should've been up on a pedestal for you. I'm a man. And I made a mistake. Maybe."

She stayed with him. Even though she was furious. Awaited the results of the test. And when they came in, he didn't know if he was relieved or filled with shame.

Because the child was his; there was no doubt about it.

And Birdie was right. He was now the villain in the piece, and there was no other way to look at it.

He, who had always tried to be a hero in one manner or another, had failed on that score, horribly. There was no way around it.

And now he had to go and face her. And tell her that she was going to marry him.

"What is that look on your face?" Emerald asked.

"I have to take another queen who hates me. And I cannot waste another moment."

"I would gently suggest that you not go in making demands to someone you have already treated so appallingly."

"I must make this final demand," he said. "I have no other choice. My child cannot be born a bastard, and she has to be my wife."

"Or, hear me out," Emerald said. "You could practice being decent."

"There is no decency when it comes to matters of the throne and succession. I will find it later."

"Will you? Because I thought that you were going to find something nice with Circe at some point, but you never did."

"How dare you? My marriage is off-limits."

"All of this needs to be within bounds, Onyx, because somebody needs to speak to you directly. Somebody who doesn't fear you."

"Apparently nobody fears me. Did you not hear all of the things that Birdie said to me?"

"Well. I'm not sure if I like you at the moment. But I have a feeling I'm going to like her."

"I don't need you to like me. I don't need anyone to like me. I have to lead this country. And I will do it now."

He stormed out of the office, and up the stairs. And then he realized he didn't actually know which room they had installed Birdie in, which meant that he was sent down the corridor, knocking on empty rooms. And by the time he arrived where she was, he had never been so angry.

She made a noise, and he shoved the door open, not waiting for her to tell him to enter.

"The test was positive. The child is mine."

She sat on the edge of the bed, her face pale, and he could tell that she'd been crying. But she looked at him with all of the steel that he knew was inside her. "You might be surprised by that. I'm not. But thank you for letting me know."

"There is no question now of the path forward."

"And what is that?"

"You will marry me. You will be my wife."

"Will I?"

"You know it makes sense. You know it is the only thing that makes sense."

"I thought I knew what made sense. And I will tell you, I thought that night that we…"

"What did you think? Were you afraid to say no?"

He was angry, and this feeling of shame wounded his pride, but he was going to be clear on this. Because if she had felt coerced in any way…

"No," she said. "I wasn't. I wasn't scared to say no. I wanted you. I had opinions on who you were, from working for you. But I suppose in much the same way that you didn't know me, I didn't know you. I very much regret to say."

"Good," he said. "But you didn't feel coerced."

"Why? Is that the one thing that would've made you feel guilty?"

"It would've been important to me. I am not a man who would ever abuse my position of power to—"

"You would never abuse your position of power to get a woman into bed, and I do believe that, but what is this if not an abuse of power?"

"It wouldn't matter if I lived in a hovel, and had no title to my name, you are carrying my baby. And I would've taken you regardless. Because no child of mine is going to grow up without me."

"You haven't exactly covered yourself in glory in all of this."

"I'm well aware. Thank you."

"You expect that I'm going to marry you?"

"Yes. You will marry me. Because if you don't, I will take the necessary steps to take the child from you, and I will find someone else to stand in as that child's mother, and you will have no power against me."

It was the most despicable thing he had ever done, the most vile thing he had ever said. But he had no other option. He had power, and he was going to abuse it in this moment. Because the stakes were too high. He didn't think that he would ever have to do that, because he knew that she would respond to the threat. He was everything he had ever despised. Everything his father had never been. A bully of the highest order.

All because he had created a situation that he had no other way to get out of. He had allowed his emotions to cloud everything. And that was the truth of it. He had been too afraid to believe in the connection between the two of them. Too afraid to believe that there was any sort of good intent behind her hiding herself and the pregnancy all this time.

And so, he had begun this as a monster, and he would have to finish it that way too.

The disdain in her gaze scorched him. "I'll marry you. But God, I wish you hadn't done this. Do you have any idea how it could have been?" Her lower lip trembled, and she looked away from him. "But no. I guess it couldn't have been. Because this is who you really are. *This* is who you really are. You are a man who gives no quarter. You have no faith in the people around you, and you definitely don't trust yourself. Not what you feel, not what you want. And so, maybe it is a good thing that you handled it this way, because I got to see the very worst of you from the outset."

"It remains to be seen if it was the worst of me," he said. "But I do suppose we'll find out."

"And when will the wedding be?"

"As soon as possible. You're visibly pregnant, there is going to be no hiding any of this. Everyone's going to know when we slept together."

"I can see that that is a concern for you."

"Of course it is. It's not so much a concern for me as it is…my wife's memory."

He didn't think that he imagined her face softened just slightly. "I didn't know your wife well. But what happened that night, on my end, had nothing to do with disparaging her memory."

"No. It didn't for me either."

He didn't like sharing his feelings with her, and he could see that she wasn't going to share hers with him either. She was guarded now. It was his fault.

But it also worked, because he had no desire to give anything of himself.

He didn't even know what he had to give.

The only thing he could feel right now was anger. Nothing emotionally had caught up with itself. There was just that burning outrage. Though he had a feeling now it was mainly directed at himself.

"The wedding will be announced tomorrow," he said. "And will take place at the weekend."

"That's outrageous. There's no way that it can all come together in time."

"It can, and it will. Because I'm the king, and I will it."

"I hope that you know, we will never have a relationship. Not again."

"We don't need one. We already have a child coming. And so, you will be free."

And he would be trapped again. In the same sort of marriage. In the same sort of life. He'd experienced one brilliant moment of passion, and he had extinguished it. So he could take the punishment. He would have to. He would have to spend the rest of his life working toward being the figurehead that his father was. Working toward building a legacy that spoke well of his parents. They had been dead in their mid-thirties. There was very little space now between his current age and the age his father was when he died.

There was no guarantee that he had years and years to create a legacy. To do his father's legacy proud.

"Tomorrow the announcement will go out."

"Is this one of those things where we have to stand up on the balcony and make a statement? Do I have to stand behind you and look grave?"

"No. There will be no announcement. We will get

married, you will wear a gown that is discreet regarding your pregnancy, and then we will announce the birth of the child when he is born."

"Or she."

"Either one."

"People will count."

"Yes. They will. They will count, and that is just fine. But in the meantime, we will buy space from that. In the meantime, we will keep a low profile."

"Wonderful. Subterfuge. With the man of my dreams."

"You're angry with me," he said. "But now you're a queen. If you can't find something to be grateful for in that, then maybe you are never destined for much happiness."

"That will be a change. Living with someone who despises me? That just seems like more of the same."

"I don't despise you."

"And yet."

He turned to leave the room, and wondered if there was something else that he could say. There was nothing. But he knew how to live with a contentious wife.

She was right about one thing. It was only more of the same. And it seemed like the two of them had hungered for something different. Now they were going to get it. But he would have a child.

His life wasn't his own. It belonged to the kingdom.

He could accept that.

CHAPTER EIGHT

The wedding was announced, and Birdie kept her head down, and stayed in her room at the palace. It wasn't long before Elizabeth came to visit.

"Are you all right?"

"I'm as good as I can be. I'm furious at him."

"And for good reason," Elizabeth said.

Birdie sighed heavily, so aware of what she'd dragged poor Elizabeth into. "I'm glad that he didn't fire you."

"He wouldn't. I've known him since he was a child."

"Well, he's acting in a fairly egregious manner. So who can say what he might do at this point."

"True," Elizabeth said. "You're going to go ahead with the marriage?"

Birdie felt like there was glass ground into her heart. Every breath, every beat, was painful.

"I don't have a choice. It isn't about what I want, it's about what's best for my child. He's a king, Elizabeth. I can't deny him what he wants. If I don't marry him then my child won't ever be able to take the throne. And that is his legacy. His right. Or her right. It's just that…he threatened me," Birdie said, closing her eyes. "He said that he would take the baby away from me. I know he would. And I can't even be furious with him for that, because what choice would he have?"

"To not be terrible?"

"Well, he's dug the hole, hasn't he?"

"That is remarkably insightful. And perhaps a bit too forgiving."

"I don't actually want to be forgiving. I just recognize that his options are limited."

And so were hers. But she had been entirely present, and entirely willing the night they had sex.

She had disregarded any thoughts of contraception. It was her fault too.

That was the reality of it. He hadn't done it alone. And if he hadn't behaved as he had in the aftermath, then this wedding would be a joyful thing.

"I'll help you with your dress."

"Thank you," she said. "I really do appreciate it. He wants something discreet. Something that will disguise the pregnancy."

"On your petite frame it won't be that difficult. But, I question to what end."

"Because then we'll just have a baby and people will obviously talk, and speculate, but it is better than creating a shock wave because a pregnant bride is walking down the aisle of a royal wedding. In the grand tradition of heirs, you have to at least pretend."

"You're being alarmingly calm."

Birdie laughed. "I'm not calm. Not at all." She thought back to her father marrying Lady Tremaine. To his death. To her subsequent banishment to being little more than a servant in her own household. And then her taking a job at the palace.

"My life hasn't been what I wanted it to be for a very long time. At least in this role, I'll have some power. Some power to do good for the country. And more than that, my child will be taken care of."

"I suppose you're right about that."

She was doing what she could. She was trying to have courage. She was doing the very best she could.

She lost herself in the details of all of it. Through the little mundane things of every day. That she got to rest a bit, instead of working from early in the morning to late at night. That her stepmother wasn't there to criticize her, to order her around. That her stepsisters weren't there to needle her.

She focused on her dress fitting, the details of the gown, the little things. The way the fabric felt sliding over her skin, how luxurious it was. The way that it felt to slide into her bed at night, with the most glorious sheets she'd ever felt in her life. Everything about the present moment was nicer than the one she had come from. Unless she thought about Onyx, so she didn't. She separated the moment, the luxury, from anything to do with him. She thought only about the day. Every breath. Every bite of glorious food that she had.

She didn't dwell on the unpleasant things. She didn't dwell on the uncertainty.

Because there was no point.

And it was the only way that she could stay sane.

Her heart had been broken incrementally.

First when he hadn't recognized her, and then, it had begun to piece itself back together when she had gone to the ball, when he had looked at her as he had. Kissed her again.

But it had been shattered irrevocably with his distrust. And there was something galling about that too. She was getting used to it. What it felt like to live without that feeling inside of her chest, which had been there from the moment she had first developed a crush on him when she'd started working for the palace.

She knew how to love him without hope.

And now she was learning to be with him without that love.

She would.

It was all just a process.

But no part of her life had ever fit her perfectly. So why should this be any different? There was an element of comfort here. With not having it all.

Yes. She could definitely get used to that.

Because she was strong, if nothing else.

Something else she had never really given herself credit for, because she had also felt soft and vulnerable. Because she'd had romantic hopes, and that made it feel like maybe she was fragile.

But no. With a broken heart, she still stood strong. And that said something about her.

By the time the wedding day rolled around, she was so used to counting every breath, feeling every moment, that it went by slowly, deliberately, and she felt no anxiety. The dress was put on, her hair and makeup done, and she didn't think about what lay ahead.

She felt a fluttering in her stomach, put her hand on it and breathed as the baby moved within her.

That was what her life was made of. These little moments of luxury, this life growing within her.

There was beauty. As long as she looked at every moment, rather than the whole of it all.

The florist put a bouquet in her hands, brilliant lilies, all pink and grand, and she looked at those, took in the scent.

What a wonderful moment.

She was in a glorious dress; she had never looked more beautiful. She was holding a bouquet of beautiful flowers, and her baby was moving.

Whatever happened afterward didn't matter. She focused on the small things. On the ring on her left hand, which Onyx hadn't put there. It had been sent to her room, glorious and stunning. Indefinably lovely.

Beautiful.

There were so many beautiful things.

Even when your heart was broken.

She took a breath, and realized that she was outside the chapel on the palace grounds.

How beautiful. Ornate, carved stone. It was a lovely day. The sky was clear and blue, the sun high and warming. Everything was fine.

The smell of early spring, combined with her bouquet was intoxicating. Everything was fine.

She took a step into the chapel, and she focused on the stained glass. The lovely, carved wooden doors that separated her from the sanctuary.

Everything was just fine. There was nothing to be afraid of.

Nothing.

And then the doors opened, and she made the mistake of looking ahead. Not at the flagstone floor, with its brilliant carving, but all the way down at the end of the long aisle, with every seat in the place full. There was a priest. And there was Onyx. Severe in a dark suit, and staring at her. She hadn't seen him since that day he had informed her that the wedding would be taking place.

She hadn't wanted to. She had just wanted to breathe, and be.

But suddenly it didn't feel possible. Because he was looking at her. And she felt like she was going to shatter.

She tried to catch her breath, tried to be in the moment. But she couldn't ignore now that every step was taking her toward him. And she couldn't ignore the way that he affected her body, still. She had been numb to it, ever since he had come to the house to fetch her. She had been in a bubble the past few days. Or perhaps it was just shock.

Was that what the past few days had been? She had thought that it might be something like happiness. But no.

It had been denial. Denying exactly what was happening today. Doing her best not to think about it because it was the only thing that let her feel good.

Because it was the only thing that had made it feel like she could get through this.

Her legs were trembling now, and she thought that she might pass out. The way her gown flowed over her curves, it wasn't impossible to see her stomach, and maybe everybody was looking at it. Maybe everybody was looking at it, and they knew.

That she had disregarded her own safety and sanity, and touched the king, a lowly servant who hadn't any right to do that.

They would look like exactly what they were. A shotgun wedding. They would look like two people who had given into passion with no regard for anything else.

And while that had been a beautiful moment in time for her, it didn't feel like it now. It felt scalding and embarrassing. It felt like the end of her.

It felt like dying.

Every breath now felt like it was closer to the last one she would ever take, and that felt perilously close to dying.

No. You're not dying. You have a child to think of. You have a country to think of. And you have yourself to think of.

Whether it was denial or not, she had felt some form of happiness these past few days, and she would cling to that. She wasn't meant to be miserable forever. Nobody was.

There was always hope. She wasn't going to discard it now.

When she reached the head of the aisle, he extended his hand toward her, and her breath caught. He had touched her that day that he had taken her from her stepmother's house. But it hadn't been gentle. It hadn't been like when they had touched that night in the study. This wouldn't be either.

But it felt significant. Slowly, she let him take her hand. His own was large, calloused and strong. He wrapped it around her fingers, and held onto her tightly.

"Let us begin," the priest said.

He was saying words, but she was busy focusing on Onyx. She had done her very best not to think of him. Not to imagine him. And now there he was. Looking at her with those fathomless, dark eyes, his mouth set into a grim line. She tried to find something in his expression that reminded her of her lover from that night. But she couldn't see it.

Maybe it was foolish to look for it now. What would it change?

What would it change?

Well, it might give her the assurance that he was all of these things. The hard, difficult man who had become a villain to her when he didn't trust her, but also, the passionate lover who had given her the kind of pleasure she had only ever dreamed of before.

Without love, did it matter? Because that night she had given herself to him out of something much deeper than lust.

But maybe it didn't have to be that way. Maybe she could just enjoy his body. Maybe, if she didn't want to hold on to her anger they could build something a little bit more like…

No. This was the danger of thinking of the future. She grounded herself in the moment, in her breathing. In him. That was the problem. The thing in front of her right now was Onyx.

She realized now that he was a stranger to her.

That was the real lesson. The one that she had been resisting.

It wasn't that she had known him before, and then he had changed. He contained multitudes. The ability to make her sigh out with pleasure, and make her weep.

He was hard, and he was soft. He was good, and he could do very bad things.

He could be a man respectful to the one who served him his coffee every day, and he could be a vicious snob.

He would defend his territory, would make it clear that he was not to be trifled with when he felt that he needed to.

Onyx was something much more complex than she had ever allowed him to be. He had been a king that she loved. And she had been a servant. He had been married, out of reach for so many reasons, and now she had to actually contend with the reality of him. So far that reality was difficult. So far that reality was something she wanted little to do with.

And now she was going to have to face it. Head-on. "We will now say vows. Onyx, repeat after me."

And Onyx did. In low, certain tones, and she was listening to try to divine if there was truth to it, or if this was only ceremony.

Because with him it could be either.

When she spoke the words back, she had to make a decision of her own. Ceremony. It would only be ceremony, these promises. These pieces of herself that she had to give away to this man forever and ever so that she could have her child, so that she could have some peace.

And yet it shifted. Because she found herself digging deep and making those promises for real.

Not so much to him, but to herself. To her child.

That she would try to devote herself to this, to this role, with real sincerity, to try to make a place of happiness and security.

She wished that it didn't feel profound. She wished that it didn't feel like she was giving herself to him, because she was still angry, and she didn't feel that he deserved it.

But it wasn't about what he deserved. It was about what was real.

This moment was real. This wedding was real.

"I do," she said. And then, it was time for them to kiss. There had been no discussion of this, because there had been no discussion of anything. He moved his hand around to cup her head, and she remembered that night vividly. The way that his fingers had moved through her hair. And then the ball, when they had done the same. It was the way that he held her; maybe it was the way he held all women when he was about to kiss them. Maybe there was nothing special about it, but it felt singular. And as his lips touched hers, she was transported back to that moment. Transported back to the very first time.

She had been so convinced that there was no hope left inside of her. But it began to stir. She felt the pieces of her heart begin to rattle. Felt some sense that maybe, just maybe this was still between them.

No. You don't need this.

She told herself that sternly, and then, she was the one who broke the kiss, which likely shattered all manner of protocol, and she had no idea how it looked to the people sitting in the chapel.

She hadn't thought about them even once. Hadn't looked out to see who was watching the two of them get married. She had wondered about it for a moment. And then no more. They were pronounced then, and Onyx held her hand as they walked down the aisle together. There was no reception planned for the day, and she was grateful for that when Onyx turned to her. His expression was stern, and forbidding.

"It is done," he said.

"Yes. It is."

"I will leave you. There is a new room being prepared for you. You will be taking the queen's quarters now."

"Oh."

"They adjoin mine, but do not fear. I will not take advantage of the door between the two rooms."

"No. I suppose not."

"I didn't when Circe occupied them either."

Of course. Because she was the second of his queens to occupy the space. And he hadn't…

He hadn't used her door either.

She frowned. She wanted to ask him questions, but she knew that he wouldn't welcome them. She knew that it wasn't anything he would want to speak of. At least not to her.

And meanwhile, she was nothing but the replacement queen. And only because she was carrying a baby. If not for that, then she wouldn't be here at all.

She allowed him to lead her to the quarters, but he didn't touch her when they walked. It was in a distant wing of the palace, one she had never been in, because that wasn't part of her job. She walked into the room, which was ornate, filled with bright colors, and she felt her stomach pitch, because obviously it was Circe who had decorated this room, and Birdie had slept with the woman's husband the night of her funeral.

"You may make any changes that you want," he said.

"Oh."

"This is your room now. You're not obligated to leave anything the same."

"All right."

It felt wrong to make changes. It felt like she was erasing this other person whose position she had already taken. And everybody was going to know exactly how it happened. Maybe they would even think that she and Onyx had been having an affair.

But they hadn't been. That had to matter.

Still. There was something entirely uncomfortable about the idea of both living in Circe's space, and erasing her from it.

Her throat felt prickly.

"I have some things to see to."

"On your wedding day?"

"The world doesn't stop spinning for any reason."

"Right. I suppose that's true."

"We will have to take dinner together. It is simply expected."

"Oh."

"I will see you tonight."

"Yes. See you tonight."

She didn't really like the still sadness of this. The formality. It was almost worse than anger.

It was. It was worse than anger.

Because at least anger had something to it. This just felt…

Don't think about it. Just think about the moment.

Except, in the moment, she was surrounded by all of these things that made her feel so…wrong.

So she decided to change her clothes and go down to the kitchen. Because at least there she felt comfortable.

CHAPTER NINE

In the three days since his marriage he had barely exchanged a handful of words with his wife. He made sure that he was busy with work while they ate dinner. And she sat in stony silence as she ate her own meal.

It reminded him very much of his previous marriage, and in that case, it was easy for him to slip into the rhythm of it.

"You're going to have to take a honeymoon," Emerald said, bursting into his office without preamble.

"Excuse me?"

"There are rumors. A lot of them. And I just feel that if you don't pause and take some time off, they're going to persist."

"And what rumors are those?"

"There are rumors about everything. Of course, there is already talk that she's pregnant. And within that, there are people that are saying she was a surrogate for you and Circe, and the baby isn't even hers. That you're trying to cover that up. There are people that are saying she's your mistress. And, of course, there are people who have it right. That you got her pregnant, and had to marry her, and that's why you've done it so quickly, but that you don't know her or love her. Evidenced by the fact that you didn't even bother to have a reception."

"Neither she nor I are actors. It would have been a foolish thing to attempt."

"Still. You maybe should have. Because now you're left with a whole lot of speculation about the irregularity of everything."

"Maybe I don't care about the irregularity."

"That's a lie. You do. I think at the very least you need people to believe that you love her. Or at least you can stand to be in the same room as each other. And I know that Lady Tremaine might have signed a nondisclosure agreement that you sent over, but the staff doesn't work on nondisclosure. They spread rumors. That's why we act with a certain amount of discretion. But within this house, people are talking. And eventually some of that is going to get out."

"No one ever said anything about Circe or myself."

"Yours was a diplomatic union. Everyone knew it. This isn't. You've married a commoner. I did the same, while pregnant. You and I are beginning to look like… well, like we can't really control ourselves."

"I fail to see how your failings should reflect on me."

"Failings. I mean, really I am only human. And Andrei is…"

"Thank you. I don't want to hear about your sex life with my best friend. I'm happy you're happy."

He wasn't entirely sure he meant it. He wasn't sure if anything made him happy at this point. He was going to be a father in only three and a half short months, and all of this was insult to injury. He had to figure out how to manage the rumor mill. And his sister was right. It was better if people thought that it was a love match. A diplomatic match that was cordial rather than passionate was at least expected.

But this…

Well, it was beginning to look irregular.

"All right. I'll take her to a private island where nobody can take photographs of her. But we are going to have to seed the rumor that we'd gone somewhere without saying where. Because we can't have photographs released, because she will be visibly pregnant in anything other than a billowing gown."

"Noted," Emerald said. "I believe Andrei has just the bolthole."

"He has more secret properties than the one that he spirited you off to in Romania?"

"Yes. He's the son of a notorious crime lord. He loves a secret hiding place. Though he resented it when I said it was like having secret clubhouses like a little boy." She smiled. "I paid for that." Onyx grimaced. "Anyway he doesn't need them now. You can take her there, and the house is huge. You won't even have to see her, but everyone will believe that you're having some kind of intimate escape."

"Perfect."

"How nice that I've earned your praise."

In a bad mood, because his sister had been right, he went to find Birdie. She was not in her room. And it took him ages to track her down, by asking staff. He found her in the kitchen, stirring a pot, and chatting to the head of the serving staff. The woman who had yelled at him like he was a child and not a king. Elizabeth.

"What are you doing here?"

"Visiting," she said, stepping in front of Elizabeth like she had to protect her from him.

"I need to speak to you."

Elizabeth looked at him, one gray brow raised. "Good to see you too, Your Highness."

"Is it?"

"Nice to still have my job anyway."

"Don't push it."

He gestured for Birdie to follow him.

"We're going away on a honeymoon," he said.

She stopped. "We are?"

"Yes. We are. It is in our best interest to try and make this look as real as possible. By which I mean, we need to make it look like it is an emotional connection. If we can do that…if we can do that, then it may do something to quell the rumors that are beginning to bubble up."

"Rumors?"

"Many of them true."

"I see."

"So we're going off to a private island. My sister is arranging everything."

"Oh." She had a very strange look on her face. "I've never been out of Basilia."

"You haven't?"

She shook her head. "No. When would I have ever gone?"

"I… I don't know."

He realized that beyond a very basic biography he didn't really know anything about his wife. He knew that she was a maid. He knew that she wasn't nobility. He knew that her stepmother was…a disgusting woman. But he didn't know anything about her life beyond that. She had never traveled. He spent his life on private jets, going to many of the world's most beautiful places. Often for work, yes, but he was able to enjoy the beauty of a place.

"I will have the staff pack your things for a warm climate."

She frowned. "I'm still not used to having people do things for me. I'm not sure how I feel about it."

"Does it matter how you feel about it?"

"Well. Yes. I would say that it does. I'm still trying to get my bearings. Still trying to get a handle on all of this."

"So am I."

It was a strange, honest thing to say, and he wasn't certain how he felt about it once it exited his mouth.

"But you were born into this."

"I was. But I did think that I would have a bit more time before I had to assume the throne."

"Oh. Well. Of course." She almost looked…sympathetic. Maybe she didn't hate him quite so much as she wanted him to believe.

Or maybe she did. It didn't really matter. It didn't.

Within the hour, they were on his private jet, with her looking round-eyed and uncertain as the plane took off.

"What?"

"I've never been on a plane."

"How is that possible?"

"Poverty?"

"Your father was a businessman. Before he died. You didn't do any traveling?"

She shook her head. "No. He often traveled for business. But he didn't have any time to take me anywhere. I usually stayed with a nanny. And then, he got married and I would stay with my stepmother. Or a nanny who would take care of my stepsisters and me."

"And then?"

"Well, then he died. I'm not certain if you were able to pick it up from context clues or not, but my stepmother doesn't see me as part of the family. Also, before he died he lost…he lost very nearly everything. All we really have is that house. It's been hand-to-mouth as far as keeping everyone fed and clothed."

"Your stepmother and stepsisters look both well clothed and well fed."

"They were receiving my salary from the palace."

"What?"

"I was seventeen when I started working there. My stepsister's the one who arranged the bank account, and got everything established for me. I had the money deposited into her account because she was the one managing the household anyway. And as she pointed out, they were the ones who needed it. Then, my stepsisters did start earning money as influencers online. Though it isn't steady. But sometimes there's quite a bit of money. A bonus, or really good brand deal. They've been sent on holidays as long as they would film it."

"But of course you were never taken on those holidays."

"No. Much like you," she said, leveling her gaze at him, "when they look at me they see a commoner. There really is no way around that. It's what consumes them. I don't deserve any of this."

He gritted his teeth. "I'm not a snob."

"You are. But it's all right. You can hardly help it. You're a king, after all. I would think that being a snob is in your DNA. And truly, royalty is in your DNA, so I suppose if given an ideal world, you were always going to try and give your child fine blood coming from both parents."

"No," he said. "That's not it. I married for diplomatic reasons. It had nothing to do with my wife's bloodline. It was everything to do with the connection."

"Which is blood by extension."

"If you like," he said.

"It's not about what I like or don't like. It's true."

"They were cruel to you," he said.

"No more or less than you."

"Am I being cruel?" He gestured around the private plane.

"No. But you're only taking me on this trip to save face."

"Did you need it to be personal?"

"Hardly. I'm just pointing out that it feels a little bit…a bit disingenuous for you to be unhappy with my stepmother about anything, when you haven't treated me much different."

"And what would you like from me? An apology? Would you like me to prostrate myself before you with abject humility?"

"No, of course not. I don't think you're capable of such a thing."

Circe hadn't pushed back with him like this. She had been cold, and she had been uninterested in engaging with him often, but it hadn't been like this.

Birdie was, for no real reason he could discern, completely unafraid of the consequences of speaking out of turn.

"The truth is," she said, "I was ready to run away from you. I was ready to start my life over with nothing. If you hadn't come for me, that's what I was going to do."

"Is that why you speak to me like you have nothing to lose?"

"I don't really," she said. "It's just been too many years of being treated like I don't matter. It's been too many years of having to live with people who would rather I weren't there. This is what I was trying to tell you in the limousine that day. I'm going to be a mother. And the one thing that my father could not do for me, at any point, was put me first. Was make sure that I was living in a house where I was treated well, or where people were really nurturing me or taking care of me."

She took a deep breath and he could see real hurt in her eyes, but also clarity. "He hid behind his busyness. Behind his position. But at the end of the day, the thing he cared most about was himself. The thing he cared about was his own comfort. I won't do that to my child. And so if that means that I'm going to stand firm with you, then I'm going to. Because part of that is not being treated like an incidental. My child will have a good role model. Because that is the thing, my stepmother wasn't very nice to my father either, and he just took it. That was what I learned. To take it." She shook her head. "I cannot and will not instill being a doormat as a virtue, not in my child."

"I don't think I ever suggested that you should be

a doormat." He was offended by the mere suggestion. "Did you ever meet my wife," he said.

She made a small sound. "Yes. I did. She was a very fierce woman."

"Yes," he agreed. "She was. Why would you think that I require something different from you?"

"Because you don't love me. You don't even trust me. You thought that I was lying to you about the baby."

Something uncomfortable stirred in his stomach. "My marriage to Circe was not a love match."

She blinked rapidly. He regretted saying that. It was dishonorable to her memory. And he certainly shouldn't have said it to this woman that he barely knew, this woman that he'd slept with the night of Circe's funeral, which was the height of disrespect in ways that he still felt so ashamed of.

"Oh," she said.

"It was diplomatic," he said. "Though, do not mistake me, I appreciated her. Her fire, her mind, her ferocity. The two of us may not have been emotionally attached to each other, but we were united in a common goal. I did not require her to give me fealty, I did not require her to do anything for me. What I required of her was that she be an exemplary queen."

"And yet you treat me like I'm nothing, and I'm forced to assume it's because of where I come from. If you didn't love Circe, and that's not the source of your admiration for her mind, for the way that she acted, then I'm forced to assume that the truth is you don't believe a woman born to my station can be smart with her stubbornness. You called me manipulative. That's your big fear. That a low-born woman might have manipulated you."

"I don't think any man relishes the idea that he might have someone else's child foisted off upon him."

"You believe the worst of me."

"I had no reason to believe the best of you."

"I've served you, in the palace all these years, and you thought that I was simply lying in wait to take advantage of you? I would rather be free. I've never been on my own. I've never been able to live my life on my own terms. Do you think that I crave power? I don't. That night, when I went to you, I saw a grieving man, and I wanted to comfort you. I was not plotting anything. It was nothing more than real, that moment. And you've destroyed it. Desecrated the memory of it because of your shame."

Her words hit him, square and true in the chest, and he had no good response to give her. He was treating her like she had a stake in the shame, and that wasn't fair. It was his own, and not a reflection on her, but it was real all the same. "I do feel shame about it. Because my wife deserves better. Deserved better than for me to find myself in the arms of another woman the night of her funeral because I was free of our vows."

He felt bad about saying that. And yet it was true. Still, though, it seemed a poor thing to say. And he could see that reflected in her gaze.

"Then your anger is with yourself," she said. "And you've turned it on to me. But I've had my fill of that, thank you very much. So I won't be there to be a surrogate to your self-loathing."

She moved away from him then, sitting in a far corner of the plane, curled up and ignoring him.

It was all for the best. He didn't know what to say to her. When they landed, there was a car waiting for them at the runway.

"This isn't an airport," she commented.

"No. This is a private island. Owned by my brother-in-law."

"He's quite mysterious," she said.

A strange spike of something hot hit him in the chest. "Not really. He's the son of a Romanian crime lord."

"Really?"

She sounded genuinely interested and he found that irritating.

"Yes," he said. "Really."

"That must be appalling to you," she said.

"Why would it be?"

He got into the driver's seat of the car. There would be no staff on the island while they were here. Everything was in place for them, meals had been preprepared and supplies had been delivered for the period of time that they would be taking their honeymoon, but they would be isolated. It had been at his request. He did not need an audience for this prison sentence with his little maid.

"Because you're deeply snobbish."

"Andrei is and has been like family to me all of his life. I don't care who his parents were."

"You certainly care about who mine were."

"No," he said. "I don't." She was right. That was the problem. She was right about the fact that what he really hated was what this said about him. That what he really despised was his own weakness reflected back at him in her eyes. The way that she made him feel even now.

He had been angry, ever since he'd discovered her at the ball, but it wasn't at her. It was him.

The way that he had let himself obsess about her. The way that he had become so…frail. So human.

It was something he had never been allowed to be, and he had flung himself into it, and it had been the easiest thing in the world to leap to the worst conclusion possible so that he could push those feelings away. So that he could discount them.

It was easier to believe that she had put some kind of spell on him than it was to believe that he was just a man. One who had been held captive by his cock.

It was beautiful on the island. He was having difficulty taking it in. She sat in the passenger seat, looking out the window, deliberately looking away from him, and he started up the engine, the car purring to life.

The GPS in the car was programmed to take them to the house, though Andrei had told him that it was all very basic because there was only one road that went all the way around the island, and another one that led up to where the house sat, perched on the only high elevation that the island possessed.

He was out of his element, out of his comfort zone. And that was a very strange experience.

He was used to having staff, not used to being isolated like this. If he traveled it was typically for diplomatic events. He didn't take vacations. Certainly he had never gone on a trip like this with Circe.

For one, brief moment, he had the realization that he and Birdie were suddenly on equal footing.

She had never been here; neither had he. There would be no staff, no servants. Nothing to put her more closely in their category and not his.

Was he a snob? It was quite a snobbish thought to have, he supposed.

When they reached the house, he parked the car in front of it. It was beautiful. Very unlike the palace. Modern and made of heavy, dark concrete, the windows large and expansive. It looked like a continuation of the mountain. The same black-lava rock color all around them. The bottom floor was completely shrouded by the jungle surrounding them. And the second floor rose up above the palms, likely offering beautiful, circular views of the glorious Caribbean Sea.

There were cracks in the concrete, naturally occurring from the elements and from shifting; moss and vines had begun to grow around and in them. It had the look of an ancient temple, and he felt a quiet whisper in his soul that was something like reverence.

He looked at Birdie, and saw that the expression on her face was reflecting much the same thing.

It was…off-putting to say the least. To experience such a unified response to this woman who…

He didn't like the way she made him feel.

That was what it came down to. It was inconvenient. And it had nothing to do with his running of the country.

Nothing to do with the legacy that he was chasing.

"I believe we will find the inside completely outfitted for our use."

He looked at her, and then away. There was something about the clarity of her blue gaze that bothered him.

"Wonderful," she responded.

Then she did some thing wholly unexpected. She walked ahead of him, and directly into the house without deferring to him, without waiting to see what he would do.

He followed behind her, but she was already halfway up the floating staircase at the entrance of the house when he got in.

"Where are you going?"

"I'm going to find my bedroom. I assume it will be the one with the women's clothing in it. I would like a reprieve. And I would like perhaps to explore the island."

"I…" He found himself speechless. He couldn't remember the last time that it happened. He had a feeling it was around her, though, and he didn't care for that at all.

"There's no one here," she said. "We have no need to perform. Even less than we had a reason to perform when we were in the palace. I find that cheering. Don't you?"

He couldn't say that he found anything cheering. Not at this particular moment. But before he could open his mouth to say it, Birdie had vanished up the stairs, and he heard the opening and decisive closing of the door. The click of a lock echoing through the empty house.

For the first time in his memory, Onyx had been firmly told exactly where he stood.

And it was on incredibly unhallowed ground.

CHAPTER TEN

THE ROOM WAS BEAUTIFUL. The windows faced the impossibly blue water, a view unlike anything she had ever seen before. The bedroom was glorious. Not a tiny attic in a corner, not some other woman's quarters, but airy and bright. The bed was plush, with white pillows and a white duvet. There was a hand-woven rug on the floor made with what appeared to be natural dyes, the geometric pattern on it intricate and artful. She opened up the sliding door that led into the bathroom. There was a massive, deep tub right next to a floor-to-ceiling window. Because of course there was no reason one couldn't bathe in front of a window here. The only people on this island were the two of them. There was no one else around for miles.

There was a shower in the room as well, with a large rain head, and vines growing up the side of the interior. Making it like being caught in rain in the rainforest. She went inside and turned that water on. Let it hit her cold, stood there until it warmed up. And she cried. Because she hated all of this. Because she felt raw and bruised. Broken. Because she was too thin, in spite of her growing pregnancy, because she just couldn't eat.

Because this man was the epitome of a thwarted dream, and she hadn't realized how much that would affect her.

She could step back and be impressed by her own strength if she took the time. But there was just something so crushing about losing this fantasy. For so many years, Onyx had been a bright spot in her life. He'd been the most beautiful man. An ideal in so many ways.

But the reality of him was disappointing.

King Onyx *had* been the ultimate fantasy.

Maybe he had been a kind of escape for her in her mind.

A secret garden that only she could go to. While she had cleaned, she had imagined that she was doing this good work for him. That he would care. That it mattered. And somehow in her mind she let herself forget that his wife existed. She let herself believe that he was the sort of man who would see her, not the position that she occupied. And he wasn't.

He wasn't interesting or surprising. He was everything she had always feared a man in his position could be.

Cold, dismissive, suspicious of anyone who didn't have the power and money that he did, whatever he said.

He attempted to try and convince her her that he didn't feel that way. That it wasn't an issue, but she knew that it was.

The way that he had spoken about that night…

God, but it was so hurtful. And why did he have the power to harm her even still? She cried and gave thanks that the water was running down her cheeks, that it let her pretend that maybe she wasn't this pathetic. That she wasn't weeping piteously over this man who didn't seem to care about her at all.

Even bringing her here was all about optics.

She got out of the shower, turning the water off and drying herself a bit more fiercely than was strictly required.

But the scrub of the towel over her skin grounded her. Reminded her of exactly what was happening. Didn't allow her to get too comfortable in her glorious surroundings.

She went to the lovely armoire in the corner, opened it up and looked at all of the fabulous dresses that were hanging there. Then she opened up the drawers in the massive chest of drawers that stood in the other corner of the room. There was no closet. Likely because of the way the house was constructed, with most of the walls being made of glass.

She found a bathing suit, and a flowing cover-up. She put it on, and looked at herself in the mirror, frowning at her thinness that contrasted with her rounding belly. Her breasts, she would admit, looked amazing. She had pregnancy hormones to thank for that. Too bad nobody was going to enjoy the look of them.

There was a pair of sandals exactly in her size, with gold cross straps and soles that seemed sturdy enough for her to walk in. And she decided she really was going to go exploring. She held her breath on her way out of the bedroom, down the stairs and out of the house. She didn't want to run into him.

She needed a break from that man. And from her own ruminating about him.

He was her husband. It was the weirdest thing.

She was his queen, and that should feel like a dream come true, but it didn't. She was being absolutely honest with him when she said she had never dreamed about being queen.

What she had dreamed about was loving him. What she had dreamed about was him loving her.

What she had dreamed about was apparently actually the most impossible thing in the entire world. Because if she, Birdie Matthews, could ascend from kitchen staff to queen, but could not secure his affection in any regard, that said something about the actual state of the world.

It really and truly did.

She didn't encounter him, thank God, and instead was greeted only by the pleasant humidity, and the clinging warmth in the air when she went outside. She decided to push all thoughts of him aside. She had never been anywhere like this before. She had never traveled before. Today she rode on her first plane.

All of this didn't have to center on King Onyx. He was used to being the center of everything. He was central to Basilia, it was true. And so there was reason to his rather unavoidable inborn narcissism, but she didn't have to cater to it. She was a whole woman without him. She had been before. She was going to be a mother.

She found herself finally being able to get back to that place of total mindfulness. The one that she had found before the wedding.

This place was beautiful. The air, the breeze, the sound of the water.

She was elated to be here, actually. Maybe not with him. Maybe she felt emotional and everything was painful when she thought of him, but everything wasn't pain. Not if she didn't make him her North Star.

She was her own North Star.

She wanted freedom. And so she would claim all of the freedom that she could in this moment.

She poked around the perimeter of the house until she found a walking trail that led up the side of the hill and into the trees.

She could hear the sound of a waterfall in the distance, and she walked up farther, and came around a slight bend, and stopped. Her heart slammed into her chest as she looked down. Down and down. She was at the top of the man-made staircase, craggy stone steps extending down more than fifty feet into what looked like a fortress. Large stone walls built up on either side of a pathway. There were trees down there, hanging vines. It was unlike anything she had ever seen before. Beautiful and glorious. Like something from another world.

She gripped the handrail, and began to walk down the stairs slowly, listening to the sounds all around her. The birds. The wind in the trees. The ocean waves, a persistent sound even this far away from the shore.

She smiled.

There was magic. There were still miracles.

Onyx and his attitude didn't get to take them from her. Didn't get to decide how happy she was.

Right in the middle of that bubble of happiness she felt tired. Because hadn't she been playing this game for far too long? Hadn't she been trying to be happy in the face of other people's misery for far too long?

She had been relentlessly optimistic in the face of her

stepmother's hatred and subjugation. When her stepsisters had been dismissive and awful to her, she had done her best to focus on who she was and what she was doing. She was having to do it again.

But at least you know how. You were made for this.

That was an indescribably sad thought, and yet, it was real. And true. None of this was fair. But no aspect of life had ever been fair. Why would it start now?

It wasn't fair that Circe was dead. She had been young and vibrant. It wasn't fair that for all he was king, Onyx was a man with his heart locked behind a wall.

And so there was nothing to be done. She could acknowledge all day long that it wasn't fair that she was back in this position yet again. That she could never seem to escape it.

But there was nothing to be done. Nothing to be done but live it as happily as possible.

And God knew that through the years many women had to make these bargains.

Had to find ways to be happy in situations they wouldn't have chosen.

She wasn't unique.

Her sadness didn't make her special.

Her determination to find joy—that might make her special. And if it didn't, then it would perhaps make her a good mother. That was something that she cared about. The truth was, tragedy was common. This wasn't a tragedy. She was comfortable. She would have everything she needed to raise her child.

She was on a private island.

She refused to be despairing.

She made it to the bottom of the staircase, and looked

up, feeling tiny, dwarfed by these massive stone walls. The pathway was made of rocks, the masonry beautiful and ancient. She wondered what the history of the island was. It must've been populated at one time, or why would this exist?

She followed the stone path, where it wound around the corner, the sound of a waterfall growing louder and louder. And then when she rounded the next corner, she stopped. The waterfall crashed down from the very top of the stone wall in front of her, into a pool below that seemed to flow around the path that she was standing on. Behind the walls, into a place she couldn't see.

It was like a temple.

Suddenly, she saw movement behind the waterfall, and she jumped back. It was Onyx. Wearing a pair of tight swim shorts, his glorious, sculpted body on display, his dark hair wet, pushed back off his head.

"What are you doing here?" he asked.

"I might ask you the same thing."

"I decided to have a look around."

"Do you have information on the island that I don't? Because you seem to have taken to the water easily enough. What if there are piranhas?"

"I don't think so."

"How do you know?"

"Here I am. Unconsumed. By aquatic predators, at least."

She frowned. "What is this?"

"You are correct, I do have some information on the island. I looked it up. During one of the wars there was a military base here. This was a way to move easily between bunkers. There was one where the house stands now. And there were others on the other side of the island. I believe that some of them are still there."

"Oh. I was hoping that it was a temple. Something holy. But it's just something that men made to kill each other all the easier. Honestly, as metaphors go it's a bit on the nose."

"What do you mean by that?" he asked, his voice grave.

She stared at him meaningfully. "Oh, I don't know. I imagine if we think deeply about it we might find that there is some link between wars in paradise and honeymoons as damage control."

He stared at her, those cool, dark eyes boring into her soul. She was unable to hold her thoughts inside now. But now the stakes were so high. When it had only been her dealing with the unfairness of life that had been one thing. But now she was pregnant, and she was determined to carve out better for her child. Determined that she wouldn't take the path of least resistance at their expense.

The trouble was, Onyx was beautiful. And no amount of him being awful to her changed that. He was beautiful, even when he was cruel. That seemed like a terrible trick. There were plenty of hideous-looking royals in the world, byproducts of centuries of inbreeding, that snobbery leading them down a path of distorted features and reduced intelligence.

Not so with Onyx. He was clever. Sharp. And physically perfect. His chiseled jaw, golden skin and sculpted chest were straight out of a romance novel. His body was physical perfection in every way, and it was difficult for Birdie to believe—still—even with the evidence of their passion growing inside of her, that she had ever touched him.

That she had ever been able to get close enough to him to be allowed to do so.

And by all rights, with his behavior, he should've transformed into something hideously ugly in her sight. And yet. And yet.

"There is no one here now," he said. "As you pointed out, the trip itself is about optics. But there are no optics here."

"That must be very interesting for you," she said.

"Excuse me?"

"Really," she said. And she had a full appreciation of the fact that this put the two of them on equal footing in a way that she hadn't fully considered.

She was used to blending in. What she did was the opposite of performance. She never drew attention to herself. As a member of staff at the palace, it was part of her job. As a member of her household with a stepmother who hated her beyond the telling of it, it was a matter of survival.

The one time Birdie had ever drawn attention to herself had been in the study with Onyx. Had been when they'd made love, and look what a disaster that had turned into.

Onyx did everything for visibility. Except that moment in the study.

In those quiet moments, when there was no one else around, she supposed they were more alike than they were different.

Maybe.

"Whatever will you do if a lift of your quizzical brow doesn't make headlines?"

"I have no desire to be a headline," he said.

"Do you not? It seems as if you do everything out of deference for those headlines."

"Deference and realism are two very different things than desire."

"If you say so."

"I do."

"And if you say so, then it is law. At least back in Basilia. But I suppose not here. Are you even a king here?"

"You are impertinent."

"I'm your wife. You only seek to remind me of my impertinence, or my perceived getting above myself because I'm a servant to you. Yet again, another strike against your snobbery."

"I'm growing weary of you."

"That is too bad."

She turned away from him, peering around the wall, where the stream was flowing. "And what's over there, I wonder?"

"Snakes, most likely."

"Are there snakes here?"

"Entirely possible."

"Interesting." She walked out ahead of him, following that stream. There were no paved walkways out beyond the wall. It was all rocks and snarls and hanging vines. There were also trees with plump, ripe fruit hanging off of them. She wasn't going to climb a tree; she wouldn't do anything half so foolish while she was pregnant. Though, she was a very accomplished tree climber from her childhood. But just reaching up to the next few branches didn't seem like it would cause very much trouble.

She climbed up onto a branch, then to the next one like it was a rung on a ladder.

"What in the hell are you doing?"

"I'm picking fruit. Because it is one of life's great joys. But then, I suppose you don't know that."

"Why would I know that?"

"Because you live in the world, Your Highness."

"I have never had occasion to pick fruit."

"Of course not. Someone does it for you. And they present it to your royal personage, and prepare a fine meal besides, and you never have to examine the how of any of it."

"You speak to me as if you find me ignorant."

"And arrogant," she said.

"Get down from there."

"I'm perfectly fine."

"You are absurd. And pregnant."

"A pair, we make then. For you are ignorant and arrogant, and I am absurd and pregnant." She reached out and plucked a fruit off the end of the branch. "And I am also in possession of a guava. You may envy me now. Something to add to your list of adjectives."

"Get down."

"If I died, you would find yourself short one problem."

And that was when he crossed the empty space between them, and gripped hold of the branch she was standing on, hauling himself upward, wrapping his muscular arm around her waist and pulling her down.

His skin was bare, slick and wet from his time in the waterfall, and he was also hot. The heat coming from inside of him, a raging inferno of intensity and hard muscle.

She did her best not to yelp as he nestled her against his broad chest and brought her back down to the ground.

"You are foolish," he said, plucking the guava out of her hands. "That's mine," she said.

He looked down at her, those dark eyes fierce. Her heart began to beat harder, faster. She became so acutely aware of where her breasts brushed against his hard wall of muscle, where his arm was wrapped around her like an uncompromising steel band. And how much it reminded her of the last time he'd held her like this. In the garden. Before he'd discovered the pregnancy. Before he'd decided that she was his enemy.

"You are silly," he said.

"I am not silly. I want a guava. I would beg that you haul your royal ass up the tree and fetch me another one, since you have stolen my bounty."

He stared at her, his expression unreadable.

"Well?"

"It is not befitting for a king to climb a tree."

"Remember, you are not a king here."

"I fear that I am a king always."

"No," she said. "Only if you want it to be true. Have you ever just been a person? Even before you were king? Were you ever just… Onyx?"

"I was the heir," he said. "There is a set of obligations that come with that from the moment you take your first breath." He stepped away from her. "Our child will bear the same fate."

She frowned, a heavy sensation settling in her chest. "Oh. I hadn't really thought of that."

"It's the truth. Our child will meet the same fate once I die."

"Don't die anytime soon."

He laughed. "Believe me, making it longer than my father is a goal of mine."

"You became the heir when you were sixteen?"

"I did."

"So before that did you ever...?"

"Climb trees? Pick fruit? Live even a moment when I wasn't aware of the crushing weight of the responsibility of what lay before me? Not especially."

"You're not any more free than I am, are you?"

In fact, he was significantly less free. Yes, she could leave. And the consequences of that would've been a struggle. A life of poverty, most likely. But the entire weight of the nation didn't rest on her head.

Though, she supposed it did now. At least to an extent.

He turned away from her, and began to climb the tree. "Well, don't break your royal neck," she said.

"I'm not the king here," he said. "At least so I've been told. And my lady wife wants those."

"Your lady wife has behaved appallingly, and is sorry."

She didn't think she had really behaved appallingly, but she did feel bad for not really considering the reality of his life. The weight of what he carried. It didn't excuse the way he treated her, but it did excuse certain things about him. And even really acknowledging what it all meant for her child to be born into royalty was something.

No wonder he'd wanted a queen who understood.

Circe was likely ready to train a child in the ways of being royal. She was ready to submit a child to that. And Birdie didn't even know where she fit into all of this.

Maybe his feelings about her were more than snobbery.

But her thoughts were cut off from that when he grabbed the first piece of fruit, and continued on up the tree. He moved with lithe agility, his graceful athleticism a sight to behold. At least that's what she was telling herself. And not that he was an actual snack, one that she wanted badly to take a bite of. How could she still be aroused by him? It was one thing to respond to his touch. After all, they'd been intimate, and even though she was angry at him it was difficult for her to forget the pleasure that they'd shared together.

But just looking at him made her feel that way.

She was so weak. Weak and exceedingly basic. But what did it matter? She was stuck on this island with him anyway. What did her pride have to do with any of this?

So she watched him. Those thick, muscular thighs, his washboard abs and incredibly powerful biceps.

"You go to the gym every day?"

He looked down from the tree, giving her a strange look while he gathered more fruit. "Often."

"You're very athletic."

"I try to keep myself strong. Like I said, I'm trying to outlast my father. But life is cruel and brutal, and no amount of doing sit-ups every day is going to alleviate that."

"I know," she said.

"You do, I suppose. How old were you when your mother died?"

"Seven. She was lovely. At least as far as I remember. I was happy when I was with her. She loved me. You know, we aren't the same, but I relate to you in this way. For the first seven years of my life, I was allowed to be Birdie. Simply as I am. But ever since my mother died, I've had to be something else. I've had to dedicate myself to being useful for people who despise me. I had to keep my head down and be invisible in the palace. I don't really know what it's like to simply live either."

"And you won't now. Because now you're a queen." He began to climb down the tree, a bushel of guava cradled in his arm. "And you are required to present a front, as I am."

"I understand that."

"I know you do."

"But perhaps here we don't. I think that you and I need to find some common ground."

"We are on it," he said, looking down between the two of them. Where they stood, barefoot on this rocky soil.

"You know what I mean. I don't know you. Not really. There were things that I thought I knew about you because I worked for you. I will be very honest with you, I elevated you to a position that no man can live up to. I fashioned you into my perfect fantasy because it gave me something to do. And then I was shocked when you didn't live up to that."

"Well, you understand now. Why I reacted to you the way that I did."

"No," she said, laughing. "I don't. You were cruel by any metric. I can't say that I understand. But I can honestly say now that I shouldn't have been surprised. I fashioned you into a fantasy, and my fantasy man was going to understand everything that I did. He was going to see my heart. But you aren't that man. You are hard and—"

"Ignorant and arrogant. Envious, as well, so I have heard."

"Yes," she said. "And so now I've been very angry at you. But perhaps I need to get to know the man you really are. And you need to get to know the woman that I am. Especially since we're going to live together."

"I never got to know Circe."

She frowned. "Not at all?"

"No. We couldn't find common ground, as it happens. She was a good queen. She served our people. She made good changes. She hated being my wife. She didn't like me. I'm not sure that I liked her."

"Well, I can understand that. I'm not sure that I like you either."

"Good news. If my first marriage proved anything it's that two people can be married for quite some time without liking one another."

"True. But a counterpoint. I don't want to live that way. I was so exhausted earlier because I was thinking about how this is just more of the same. How I have been forced to live in homes where I'm unwanted, disliked. And here I am again. Your unwanted queen. I don't want to do it. I want us to like each other. And maybe the difference between you and I, and you and Circe, is that we do have a child on the way. I would rather not despise my child's father. I would rather he didn't despise me."

"You make a good point."

"I often do. Which you would discover if you spent a little bit less time hating me."

"I'm not sure that I hate you."

"Oh. You aren't sure. Well, how nice for me."

"Nothing is going to change the fact that my first responsibility is to the country. My second will be to the child."

Something uncomfortable shifted inside of her. "Your first responsibility should be to your child," she said.

"Perhaps in an ideal world. But this is not an ideal world. It is a monarchy. And I am unable to offer something substantially different than what was offered to me."

"Did your father put the country first?"

Onyx looked away. "My father was a wonderful man. Everything he did, was for the good of everyone. He raised me to be his heir. Raised me to be exactly what he needed me to be. I am forever grateful to him. Because he died when I was so young, and all that was left were his lessons. Yes, I am extremely grateful to have those lessons."

"Let's have dinner tonight," he said. "You and I."

She reached out and took a guava from the crook of his arm. "We could have dinner right now."

"No. I want to learn more about you. You are right. There is no reason for the two of us to be at odds."

"So everything must be a plan. You can't just be?"

"No," he said. "I can't. That is what it means to be king." He deposited the guavas into her arms, and began to walk away from her. Leaving her standing there with an armful of fruit.

"See you at dinner," she said.

She couldn't quite decide then if she had gotten the upper hand, or if she had somehow made things worse by allowing herself to see something of the actual man.

It was easier to hate him. Easier to resent him for what he had made her feel.

It was much more complicated to acknowledge that much in the same way she was, he was simply a product of everything that life had made him into.

CHAPTER ELEVEN

HE HAD NO idea what to wear to dinner. It was a very foolish thought to have as Onyx stood in the expansive master bedroom in the island home, looking around for what he might wear to sit across from his queen.

There was no one here. No one but her. It didn't matter.

He thought of the way she had looked earlier today. Wearing a bikini, a flowing cover-up thrown on top. Her breasts were full and lovely, her belly gently rounded, and he had been so aware of the fact that he had been inside of her. Touched her. Kissed her. And that all the intimacy since then had been lost, and he was left to crave it. Obsessed himself over it.

And what was the point of that? He had never in his life been obsessed with a woman, and it had been this way with her ever since they'd first touched. But it wasn't that way when she was in his study cleaning. Wasn't that way when she was nothing more than the little maid who brought him tea during the day.

The trouble was, she was more than that. It was becoming harder and harder for him to deny it. She was more than that, and what she was had taken over his life.

He growled fiercely, took a white shirt out of the closet and put it on, rolling the sleeves up. He wore a pair of linen pants with it, because he didn't need to wear a whole suit, and it felt distressingly informal. He had no idea how much a full suit had become armor for him.

He didn't know when he had begun needing armor.

Perhaps always?

Perhaps.

He was so often untested. The last time, before Circe's death, before Birdie had stormed into his life, was when Andrei had gotten Emerald pregnant and stolen her from her wedding.

He had felt out of control then, and he hadn't liked it. It was a reminder of how random life could be. When even your best friend could do something completely out of character. Or at least, out of character based on what Onyx had known of him. It was even more sobering to realize that he had never fully understood Andrei, or Emerald, and the nature of their relationship.

It had never occurred to him that while he was guarding Emerald, the two of them were pining. Desperately.

But they had been.

He didn't like being confronted by his own blind spots.

This wasn't the same. Except, it felt related. The way that he hadn't seen the maid until she had been in a tight dress, touching him. The way he hadn't understood her strength, even as he was accusing her of all manner of subterfuge.

And this, now. The way he had been manipulated into inviting her to dinner. That was what had to have happened. She had somehow suggested the notion. That they sit and eat together, get to know one another. Because he was the father of her child.

That realization made his stomach go tight. Yes. He was the father of her child. He…

He was the father of the child.

The DNA test proved that.

She'd said that she was a virgin when they were together. That she'd wanted to comfort him.

Jesus. It made him feel so appalled at himself. Perhaps that was his real problem. When he looked at her, he felt nothing but anger at himself.

For being a man who was vulnerable to those kinds of very human mistakes.

He wondered, not for the first time, what his father would've thought of any of this.

He couldn't ask him. His mother and father had married for the good of the country, and he had wanted badly to do the same. It was why Emerald had decided to enter into a convenient marriage as well.

This wasn't any different than his first marriage. No, it wasn't political in the way his marriage to Circe had been but they were having a child, and when you were royalty, there was very little that was more political than a child.

He grimaced, even as he had that thought.

But it was different to be the heir.

It was. You had to be prepared for this life.

His parents had been very warm people. Loving. But when his father had given him lessons, he had been hard and uncompromising. Had told him that it was the way the ruler of a nation had to be.

And Onyx had always been able to see the difference. That at the end of the day, a king had to be able to be the symbol before he was anything else. That he had to be able to put duty before everything.

There was no duty here, and he disliked it.

He went downstairs, and began to rummage through the fridge. There were pre-prepared boards of meat and cheese, and packaged meals with instructions on them. He tried to decide what he thought the little maid would like.

He had never really watched her enjoy a meal. Didn't really know what she would enjoy.

He decided on two very nicely prepared steaks with instructions for reheating so as not to overcook them, and buttered potatoes.

It was an elegant meal, particularly along with the cheese board. Although, his bride could not have wine, so he was obliged to get them both sparkling pear juice from a bottle in the cupboard.

He set the table for them on the terrace that was shrouded by trees, shielded from the sun.

And when he went in the house to fetch her for dinner, she was already partway down the stairs. When he saw her, his heart jumped. She was wearing an orange dress that clung to her curves. He had never seen her dressed quite like this before.

Her blond hair was loose, her face freshly scrubbed, and glowing. She was so intensely beautiful.

He had thought so when he had seen her at the masked ball. He had thought so even when she was shrouded in shadow.

But here, she was entirely different. Alive and vibrant, sun-kissed, and radiant.

"I just came hoping that there might be food," she said.

"There is food."

"Thank you. I've been thinking," she said.

She walked down the stairs, and took her arm out from behind her back, a small green fruit in her hand. "I want to call a truce."

She pressed the guava into his palm. He closed his fist around it lightly. "Why?"

"Well. Because we need to. We need to make something better than this for our child."

He nodded slowly. "I agree with you."

"Whew. That is so nice for me." She smiled. "Sorry. That was not very in the spirit of the truce, I confess. Will you forgive me?"

"Yes."

She began to walk ahead of him, and then stopped. "I don't know where we're going."

"I'll lead you."

"I believe this is where you apologize to me for accusing me of being a calculated horror."

Her words stopped him cold. "I am sorry but I was wrong about you. But I am not sorry for being first of all defensive of the throne."

"You're sorry that you were wrong? Well, that is not very in the spirit of the truce, I fear."

"It's true. I had to do what needed to be done in order to ensure that you weren't taking advantage of me in some way."

"I am very scary," she said, lifting her hands and making claws at him. When he didn't laugh, she lowered them. "Food, please."

He led her out onto the terrace, where the meal was

set for them. She looked critically at the stemware. "I can't drink alcohol."

"I know. I did not serve you alcohol. Nor did I serve myself alcohol. And there, you see evidence of your truce."

"How magnanimous."

"I try," he said, his tone dry.

She took a seat at the table, and took a sip of the sparkling beverage. "Oh. That's nice."

"I'm glad. I haven't tried it yet."

There. He thought that was rather cordial.

He sat across from her, and she looked up at him over her glass, her blue eyes glimmering with that sort of reckless mischief she always had.

At least, that she seemed to have here on the island.

She had been so different working in the palace.

"I would never have thought that you had this much spirit."

She frowned. "Excuse me?"

"I would not have thought based on watching you serve at the palace that you were like this."

"Because that was my job. Sometimes we would talk, don't you remember?"

"Yes."

He had thought that she was funny at times. Charming, even. But she was quite young, and he had been married, so he had never thought too deeply about it.

"And you came to work at the palace when you were seventeen. Your stepmother was taking your salary."

He wanted to get her biography straight, if nothing else. He could ponder the mysteries of her, her personality and his attraction to her for the rest of forever.

But if they were going to do this thing where they got to know one another, then he needed to understand exactly what all she had done before life brought her here.

"Yes," she said.

"And what made you think to apply for work at the palace?"

"What I had heard was that you were an extremely fair employer. And, I was already a maid in my own home. So I thought I might as well get paid for it. Even though, as we've discussed, I didn't get paid for it."

"And what made you decide to live with your stepfamily after your father's death?" he asked.

"Nothing made me decide it. The way that my stepmother presented it just made the most sense. And I followed her lead. It was foolish, I admit. But I didn't know better. I was very young. But it enmeshed me deeper and deeper into this family that I was never really a part of. Just a convenience. A convenience when she felt she could use me, and a burden when she decided she couldn't."

"And your stepsisters are…?"

"Influencers," she said. "That's what they do. They make videos and put them online, they get brand deals. My stepmother very much wanted one of them to marry you when Circe died."

"The likelihood of that never existed."

She laughed. "I know. And I also know that I wouldn't be here if you hadn't gotten me pregnant."

"How did your mother die?" he asked.

She looked down. "Cancer. That's why for a while I thought I wanted to be a doctor. You know, until I woke up and realized that's simply never going to happen for someone like me."

"Is that still what you want?"

She shook her head. "I don't think so. What I really wanted was to make a difference. I wanted to do something to fight against what took my mother away. But there are other ways to do that. In fact, as queen I… Am I allowed to ask for something?"

"Yes," he said.

Her face softened just slightly. "That feels very almost generous."

"I don't know that it's generous. It's only that a queen does oversee special projects."

"I think I would like to oversee funding for medical research."

"All medical research, or cancer?"

"All of it. Especially thinking of what happened to Circe. It's not just cancer that takes people."

He was touched by her inclusion of his late wife. Touched that she felt affected by the loss. That she cared.

"And I would really like it if eventually, I could sponsor scholarships. For girls like me. Who really, really wanted to do something to make a difference, but didn't have the money."

"Yes. Of course. I will put you in touch with the appropriate channels, and we can make it happen. Though, of course, you might want to focus on that after you have the baby."

"Maybe," she said. "I'm not used to doing nothing. And this has been an extraordinary period of leisure. Punctuated by moments of pure hatred, which actually does take quite a bit of energy."

"Hopefully there will be more you can do when you don't have to spend any time hating me."

She had said that she'd fantasized about him being a good man. He felt that he was a good man. One who took great care of the throne. But clearly that wasn't how she measured it. That wasn't the way that she'd imagined him. He wondered exactly how she did.

"Does that restore me slightly in your eyes?" he said. "Offering you this."

"I don't know," she said. "It's still an extension of duty, isn't it? Still part of the job of being queen. And not really anything extraordinary."

"You are so determined to find me ordinary?"

"No, just cautious. You hurt me. I had never been with a man before. And I wanted to be with you. You assumed that I was the most diabolical sort of monster, after looking at me like I was special to you, and that is not the sort of hurt that goes away easily or quickly. The truth is, I know how to endure. And so, I just will, if I have to. I promise you that. I just will."

"Is it easier than finding a way to see that when you're in my position, you tend to assume the worst of people?"

"No. I can't. You know, I fancied myself in love with you."

The words hit him with the force of a bullet. She had fancied herself in love with him. She hadn't even known him. She…

She had fancied herself in love with him, and he had done extraordinarily cruel things with that love.

It was the missing piece. The one thing that he had

never assumed was possible. The one thing he had never imagined might be true.

He had thought that it had to do with money. Power, position.

"I just wanted to comfort you. When I saw you that night. I just wanted to comfort you. It broke my heart to see you so sad, and I would've given you anything. I didn't know that it would become sex. But I was happy to give it to you. So happy. I wanted you to be my first. And then when you had the ball, I thought that I had my chance. When you recognized me in the mask, I thought I had my chance. But you don't know me. You never did. You didn't have thoughts about me, or fantasies. And that's when I realized we didn't know each other. I didn't actually love you. I can't have. Because I didn't know you. I don't know you now. I don't love you, and that's all right."

He felt like for a moment, he had almost touched the sun, and then the warmth of it was snatched cruelly away.

But of course she didn't love him. Of course. She didn't know him.

She was right about that. He didn't know her.

And love had never been something that he required in a marriage anyway.

But it definitely gave him an understanding of how deep a betrayal it had been.

She had given him her virginity, and she had done these things from a place of innocence, care, and he had treated her like a hardened criminal.

It truly was up to him to grovel. He could not defend himself.

"I am sorry. You're right. I treated you very badly. I

used you to soothe myself, and then because of my own discomfort with my feelings, I reacted badly."

She frowned. "What do you mean?"

"About my discomfort? Only that part of me knew that I should be suspicious of what happened. That I should question it. That you appeared there, ready to give yourself to me when I needed comfort. When I was starving for human touch. And so, yes, it was easy for me to believe that you had manipulated me in some way. But the truth is, I manipulated the situation. I manipulated you. I caused an immense amount of harm to us both because I wanted our encounter to be anonymous. Because I wanted you to be a gift left there for me."

"Well, neither of the truths paint us in a very flattering light. I wanted you to be the fantasy man that I made up, and you needed me to be a fantasy that you could turn on later."

It was the truth.

"But I know you a bit now. I know that you wanted to be a doctor. I know what you want to focus on is being queen."

"Is that really knowing someone?"

"I haven't actually gotten to know another person in a very long time. Not outside the scope of diplomacy."

"Well, how did you get to know Circe?"

"I didn't," he said. His voice was heavy with regret, and so was his body. "I found it difficult, and neither of us tried."

"I want to try. I know that your expectation for marriage was always something distant. But… I didn't have one at all."

"What?"

"I was going to say something about my expectations of marriage. But I'll be honest, I never really expected to get married. Much less to a king. I have no expectations."

"You did. Of me."

"And you let me down. Which is terribly sad. But it would be hard for you to let me down worse a second time."

He could only hope that was true. He wanted her to understand how high the stakes were for him here, but to do that meant exposing his marriage to Circe.

The decision to be made, he supposed, was whether to trust her or not. He'd roared into this with no trust in her at all, accusing her of all manner of subterfuge.

In this moment he needed to drop his guard.

In this moment, he needed to give her some honesty.

"I don't want to be trapped in a marriage where my wife hates me. Not again. You said something to me earlier today. You talked about the fact that you're tired. Tired of living in a house where people despise you. So am I. I can accept fault for the state of my marriage. I wasn't a good husband. I was so focused on being a good king that I know I failed her in immeasurable ways. But also, she didn't like me. And I really didn't want to be trapped in a marriage with someone who hated me. Not again. So I would very much like it if we can come to a place where you don't hate me."

"Then you need to let go."

"Of what?"

"While we're here. You need to let go of the king. And just be the man."

CHAPTER TWELVE

The next day, Birdie was still turning over her dinner with Onyx in her head. She could think of nothing else.

Not just his physical beauty either. But the way he'd actually been vulnerable with her last night. The way he'd shared with her. But then also there was his physical beauty.

Which was vast indeed.

Pretty embarrassing to admit that level of fixation with someone who thought so poorly of her. When she came downstairs in the morning, he was already sitting there eating breakfast.

She smiled. "Good morning."

"Good morning."

Last night he'd actually shared with her, and that had stuck with her. Maybe she should try vulnerability instead of just honesty.

"It's so quiet here. You know, I've never lived by myself. And I've never even really gotten to spend a substantial amount of time without people around me. I'm often by myself. Lonely in the palace, moving through and doing my chores without chatting to anyone. And then, it's the same at my stepmother's house. Everyone ignores me. Unless they need something from me. Then it's all commandments."

"I know what you mean."

She smiled. "I guess you do. Though, I would venture to say that people speak to you with a bit more deference."

"Not Andrei or my sister."

"No. I suppose they don't. I was very impressed with your sister for taking my side when you first brought me into the palace."

"Emerald is like that. And she certainly doesn't do what I say."

"No. When she left that convenient marriage you set up for her and married her bodyguard instead I think the whole kingdom was scandalized."

"I did not set up that convenient marriage for her," he said.

She was shocked by that.

"You didn't?"

"No. I would never have married my sister off to somebody that she didn't want. She did that. She was so convinced that she needed to do something to help consolidate the power in the kingdom. She wanted to make herself as useful as I made myself, at least, that's what she said. I tried to stop her, but once Emerald makes her mind up on something, nothing dissuades her. Except Andrei. Who seduced her, and got her pregnant."

"So it runs in the family."

"Getting trapped into marriage by her pregnancy?"

She snorted. "Something like that."

He was uncomfortable with the comparison between himself and his sister.

Obviously.

"I want to go explore more on the island today. Go to the beach. I found some snorkeling equipment in one of the rooms."

"Are you sure you should do that while pregnant?"

"This is my very first adventure, Onyx."

It was the first time she called him by his name like that. Not trying to wound him or strike out at him. Not trying to be difficult. But just called him by his name because that's what felt natural.

"Obviously, I will accompany you."

"You sound so excited for your afternoon at the beach."

"Recreation is—"

"Not something you usually engage in?"

"However did you guess?"

He looked very nearly amused, and she fetched some herbal tea, and fruit, and joined him at the table.

"Let's go," she said.

That's how they found themselves down on the beach, with the picnic basket, and snorkels and flippers.

He was in that very brief swimsuit again, and she would be lying if she didn't say she very much liked it.

But she didn't have to say it out loud. The water was like a bath, smooth and clear and warm. The sea life was more plentiful than she could've imagined, and she felt like she was living in a dream. It turned out snorkeling while pregnant was a lovely activity, regardless of what Onyx had said.

He stood resolutely on the shore while she swam around, looking at fish and manta rays, and it was just such a strange thing. Because it felt like a beautiful thing that this was her life, all of a sudden.

She didn't hate him.

She didn't hate him, but it was frightening to think that she could develop feelings for him again. Because at no point had he professed to wanting that. No. In fact, even though he had been perfectly cordial for two whole days now, she still felt extremely guarded around him. Like he might turn on her at any moment. It was almost as if not only did she have a lifetime of experience with that, but he had done it to her just like everyone else.

She took her snorkel off, and rolled over so that she was lying on her back, floating there in the water. She looked up at the fathomless blue sky and then stood. The water was shallow, even as far out as she was, only coming to her waist.

She looked up at him, and he looked away.

She didn't want to ask herself if he was looking at her. But unfortunately, it was then all she could think of.

She began to walk up out of the water, moving toward him. They had done a lot of talking since yesterday. She felt vulnerable. She felt like she was clinging onto the very edge of her sanity. Or maybe she wasn't. Maybe she wasn't at all.

But what she did know was that the ache for him didn't seem to want to go away. What she did know was that one thing that made sense was touching him.

Are you an idiot?

She was. She had been the entire time. An idiot for him. An idiot to believe that love and beauty existed somewhere in this world in light of everything that she had experienced.

Ever since he devastated her, she had looked at it as

a flaw. Had taken stock of her life and asked herself why in the world she thought miracles could happen.

And many of them had. She was a queen, after all. And how many maids went from cleaning the palace to living in it?

Maybe more in history than she knew about.

But it had felt like too much to imagine that they could be more. That she could have more.

He was so difficult. The only time she had ever seen emotion in him was the night of his wife's funeral. Or rage. It was only those two things. Passion. Anger.

Choose passion.

It felt so dangerous.

And yet, right then, it was also the only thing that made sense.

She cast her snorkeling equipment to the side, as she walked up out of the water, and moved toward him. And she wasn't the one who had to close the distance between them, because he did it.

He went toward her, wrapped his arm around her waist and drew her against his body. "I don't understand what it is you do to me."

He sounded angry. Well, that was right on track. She had plenty of his anger. Just like she'd had his passion. Maybe now she would get them both. Maybe now she would get them together, she would take that.

She was yearning for something. For everything, maybe. To be loved, to be cherished, to be queen, to be free. It was too much. Too much for a simple girl to hope for, but so many girls had. For so many years. All she wanted was everything. Why not?

She was already pregnant with the king's baby.

And she was tired. She was tired of not having everything.

Maybe this would hurt. Maybe her mistake was believing that she could find a way to exist without pain. That she could gather up all the good, and it would cancel out the bad.

Maybe what she needed to do was accept that there would always be danger.

Yes. There would always be danger.

She reached up and touched his face, traced the line of his high cheekbones, all the way down to his sculpted jaw.

He was so beautiful.

Her king.

Her husband.

She wasn't common, and neither were they. But they also were. And there was something beautiful in that. Just two people at the mercy of this intense need. She had to believe that he felt it too.

She had done a good job of convincing herself that for him, it had never been this. For him it had never been this driving, intense need, but rather it had been his need to escape the grief that he was drowning in.

She knew that wasn't true now.

He was sad about his wife. He grieved her, as one did any young life lost.

But it hadn't been grief borne out of passion.

It had been something else. He had been reaching out for connection, and she would take that.

She would.

Then he lowered his head, and claimed her mouth. This kiss had a different flavor than any of the ones they had shared before.

It wasn't tinged with grief. And it wasn't filled with the kind of reverence that the one in the garden had been filled with.

She had lost that. That moment of pure emotion, and it wasn't her fault.

It was his fear. She knew that. Understood it.

But she could let it go. For now.

She could just accept this, as it was.

He cupped the back of her head, and deep into the kiss, sliding his tongue against hers, one arm tight around her waist as he held her against the firm, muscular wall of his body.

Out there in the sun. No masks, no one to watch.

They weren't shrouded in darkness, weren't hiding in the shadows.

They weren't shrouded in grief.

Not in fear.

She wasn't going to have to go home to her stepmother's house tonight. She could stay with him. They could explore this.

They actually had all the time in the world. To try to sort out what this was. To try to sort out what it could be.

That was terrifying. Comforting.

Because that meant they had a lot of time to hurt each other.

But a lot of time to heal each other too.

Maybe it meant that she couldn't continue to hang onto that part of her that wanted to protect herself.

Anger, she had found, was easy. Anger insulated you. Anger kept you from being hurt. It allowed you to turn the barbs that were being directed at you onto the other person.

It had been a revelation, because she just wasn't an angry person, but everything that had happened to her in the last few months had let her brew something vile and toxic inside of her, and she had found it to be a wonderful source of strength and protection.

But it had to stop.

It had to. She had to make room for this.

And for all the endless possibilities in it.

He kissed her, his hands moving down over her midsection, moving up to cup her breast. He kissed her, like he was dying. Like there was nothing else in the world he wanted.

And she kissed him back, because there wasn't anything else she wanted.

She was every inch that girl who had come to him that first night, except this time she knew what it could cost her to push him too far. This time she knew what she was risking, and here she was, kissing him anyway.

It was legendary, and terrifying. She had never been so brave.

She tightened her hold on him, surrendering herself to the violent need inside of her.

He growled, kissing a line down her neck, down her collarbone, to her shoulder, where he nipped her.

"I need to see you," he said.

He pulled her bikini top away, exposing her breasts to his hungry gaze.

It was barely any covering, and she found herself foolishly bashful. They'd had sex. Of course, it had been under cover of darkness, and it hadn't felt quite so…

It felt risky now. In a way that it hadn't before.

It was the knowledge that she carried with her of what it meant to fall out of favor with him.

What it meant to risk her heart.

Make no mistake, she was doing that. She could pretend that it was all attraction. That what she wanted was his body. She did.

But it was more than that, and it always had been.

He held her face for a moment, his hand cupping her chin. "I'm the only man you've ever been with?"

She nodded slowly. "Yes." Her voice trembled.

"I was very rough with you that night."

She shook her head. "No. You were perfect. It was perfect. I don't need or want you to apologize for anything that happened."

He nodded, then moved his hand down to cup her breast, his thumb sliding over one tightened bud there.

"You are a revelation. You were even then. It had been so long since I'd touched anyone."

"Is that the only reason?"

He shook his head. "No. It was something else. It was something else for me. I felt drawn to you, in a way that I'd never felt drawn to another person." He paused for a moment, and it was like he was drawing the next words from deep inside himself. Like they were difficult to make himself say. "I'm not the kind of man who has one-night stands, you know."

"You're not?"

He shook his head. "No. I never cheated on my wife, even though we weren't intimate at the end of our marriage. I've always done the right thing. I've never let my body or my head run away with me. But with you I did. With you, I have no resistance. I wanted to claim that it was the moment, but I didn't want anyone else either. It's the reason I had to have the ball. I had to find you."

They were both victims of their expectations, she supposed. He had imagined her to be someone that she wasn't, and he hadn't been able to get over the disappointment when she proved it to be just Birdie.

Or maybe it was what she had imagined earlier. Maybe the biggest problem was that he hadn't actually wanted emotion this big. And so at the first possible opportunity, he had rejected it. She couldn't say that she blamed him.

He kissed her collarbone, down to her sternum, right between her breasts, then knelt down in front of her, holding her hips, looking up and kissing her stomach, before taking her bikini bottoms down and exposing her to his hungry gaze. "You are beautiful," he said, the words hard, strained. "I've never felt like this before. I've never felt so out of control for a woman. For anyone. For anything. I've never been able to be." She wanted to talk, but she also didn't. Because her body was throbbing with need, and she just needed him.

He leaned in, sliding his tongue over her sensitive flesh, licking her right where she desired him most.

He ate her like he was a starving man, and she gripped his hair, trying to brace herself in the deep, shifting sand as he pleasured her.

Oh, the things that he did to her. The things that she was willing to risk for him. It was a private island; having sex outside wasn't a risk. That's not what it was.

But her heart.

He looked up at her, as he continued to eat her, and the look in his eyes sent her over the edge. She cried out his name, digging her fingernails into his shoulders as she fought to keep standing.

Then as she melted, he grabbed her body, braced against his, and laid her down on the picnic blanket they had brought with them. With haste, he took off his swim trunks, and she wiggled beneath him, aching to get a look at his body, which she had been denied that night in the study.

"What?" he asked.

"I want to see you naked," she said.

He looked stunned, like she had hit him upside the head with a brick. "Oh."

"You're beautiful," she said, wrapping her hand around his throbbing manhood, looking at him as she slid her thumb over that hot, smooth skin.

"It's been a very long time since…" He closed his eyes.

He was wounded. He was wounded just like she was. In different ways, with different kinds of weapons, but she could see in the way that he responded to being called beautiful, that he hadn't felt desired in a very long time.

That part of this was that he simply hadn't been able to believe that she had strong enough feelings for him to be with him for the simple reason that she wanted to.

That she cared.

"Take me," she whispered against his mouth.

He growled, positioning himself between her thighs and thrusting inside of her. She gasped, arching up against him, as he took her over and over again.

Desire built deep inside her body, and when she came, she pulsed around him, squeezing him tight, pushing him over the edge too. He growled, his forehead pressed against hers as he shuddered out his orgasm, as he spilled himself inside of her.

She clung to his shoulders, out there in the burning bright sun, replete. Satisfied, and yet also terrified.

"We can't pretend that this isn't part of us," she said. "I…"

"We can't," she said.

He rolled away from her, and sat up. Then he nodded slowly. "I want you," she said, touching his shoulder. "Don't you see?"

"Yes," he responded.

He turned to her, pressing his thumb against her lower lip. His eyes blazed into hers, his voice gruff, strained. "I want you too. In ways that astonish me. Even before my marriage, I knew that I couldn't afford to carry out love affairs. I was very discreet whenever I did. I have never been undone like this. Not ever. I need you to know that. I need you to know it isn't simply because I was celibate for as long as I was."

It healed something in her to hear that.

"Well, I'm not a virgin because I've never had the opportunity. Well, I'm not a virgin anymore," she said, putting her hand on her stomach and rolling to her side. "What I mean is, there was no one who tempted me. Whatever you believe, it isn't because you were a king. You were off-limits."

"Women have tried to seduce me before. Even when I was married."

"And I didn't," she said.

He shook his head. "No. You didn't. You just talked to me."

"It made me happy to see you every day. I was okay

with that. Just seeing you. Being near you. It gave me something that I didn't have anywhere else. It's an extremely embarrassing thing to admit."

Admitting that she'd had a crush on her husband was so lowering. But then, he seemed to need to hear it, and that helped soothe some of the sting.

"It's rebuilding something inside of me," he said, reaching out and touching her face. "Which I suppose is wholly unfair given everything that I put you through. Given that I'm a king, and you…"

"I'm lowly? I am a worm?"

"You are not. You're extraordinary. I treated you very badly. I'm genuinely very sorry about it. It was foolish of me. It was cowardice. You're right. I had feelings about my own behavior and I took it out on you. You're also right that I was the one who made up an entire story that caused all of this strife." He paused for a moment. "All this time, I thought that being too soft, letting people in, that was the only way that I could cause damage. But this… I hurt you."

She realized that it wasn't so much shock that he'd hurt her that he was dealing with now, but that he cared about it. She wondered how long it had been since he'd had to take another person's emotions into account.

"I will do my best not to hurt you again," he said.

"Well, I don't know that you should try to make that promise. Because we will be married for a very long time. At least, that's the goal. And I have a feeling you and I have yet to say all the things that we have to say to each other."

"That's very pragmatic."

"I'm not actually very pragmatic. At least, I think I

don't want to be. That isn't quite my goal. I would love to dream."

"What if I told you that you could? That I care about your dreams?"

"Why? Because you enjoy having sex with me?"

"Because I'm fascinated by you." He closed his eyes. "When I'm not trying to crush you beneath the weight of my royal rage. You're astonishing, do you know that? You know how few people would have tried to comfort me with any sort of genuine measure?"

"Given that I was the only one in the study, and the only one that you had sex with that night, I suppose the answer is very few people."

"I'm being quite serious. My circle is very small. I had hoped that my wife and I… Circe and I… When I married her I had hoped that we would find at least companionship."

"You didn't."

"I didn't. And I don't know how much of that was my fault."

"I don't want you to care about me simply because you regret your first marriage."

Maybe that wasn't fair. Maybe it was the hot sun talking. Maybe it was her being grumpy and pregnant and jealous and needy. Greedy for parts of him that no one else had ever had.

"No, that's not why. I want to know more about you. I want to understand…this."

"It's called attraction, I believe. I was a virgin until six months ago, and even I know that."

"No. It's something more."

Her heart lifted in her chest, and she had to smack

it back down. Because she had to stop getting excited just because he said something that verged on kind.

He was a man, and likely, he was mainly responding to the intensity of the sex between them. It might even be what she was responding to.

Everything was all mixed up. She had a crush on him before she knew him, and now there was this, and everything was just difficult. Everything was hard to decode. So she didn't want to. She wanted to recommit to this idea that she wouldn't protect herself. That she would let herself feel all of her feelings.

Every single one of them.

"While we're here," he said. "Let's be like this."

While we're here.

"I think you'll find, Your Highness, that we have difficulty keeping our hands off of each other at the palace too."

"But there I'm a king."

He was hiding behind that. Using it as a shield. She couldn't blame him. She wished that she had something to use as a shield.

All she had was this intense, overflowing emotion inside of her chest.

All she had was that same feeling she'd had for him all this time.

"Well, Your Highness. Then let us give you a good vacation from your status."

CHAPTER THIRTEEN

THEY WERE NAKED for days. They just never put clothes on. There wasn't a reason to. He ate with her naked, bathed with her, slept with her. He had never experienced anything like this in his life. He felt like a teenager. Hungry for her, desperate to have her body on his, to have himself inside her.

He was utterly and completely captivated by her. Everything that she was.

They were at the waterfall today, Birdie standing beneath the deluge, her nipples tight, her body lush and perfect. She was gaining weight, which he was grateful for. She had become quite thin, and he knew that it was his fault.

He knew that it was because of what a bastard he'd been. And he had been.

It had been a relief, in many ways, to let himself believe that she was duplicitous. Because it meant that nothing he felt was real.

It was cowardice, through and through. That was true. And this was something else entirely. He was allowing himself to actually be on vacation. Something he had never done before. He'd certainly never had a sex vacation, which was what this was. There was no other purpose to it. No greater good. Just him wanting her, needing her, having her.

She laughed, and extended her hand toward him, and he took it, letting her draw him beneath the spray, into her arms. He gripped her chin and kissed her. Deep and slow.

Then when they pulled away he marveled at her.

"What?" She had to shout because of the water.

He dragged her back behind the falls, into the small alcove there. "You're beautiful," he said. Because sometimes he found himself without the words to express what was happening inside of him when he looked at her, so he told her that she was beautiful. She always said thank you. She always told him that he was beautiful in return.

She didn't this time. Instead, she cocked her head to the side. "And?"

He drew a blank. Not because there was nothing to say. Because there were too many things to say. What could he say about Birdie? This bewitching, maddening creature who had taken over his life?

Six months ago, he had been in an unhappy marriage. Then he had become a widower. And then she had touched him. Revived a need in him that he had forgotten. And a fear. One that grabbed him low in the stomach and haunted him, made him feel like he was being chased by the very hounds of hell. But that didn't sound like a compliment, and maybe it wasn't. It was something more. Something deeper.

Nothing that he could shout over the din of a waterfall.

She shook her head, and turned away from him,

heading back toward the waterfall, and he gripped her arm and brought her back up against his body, kissing her with everything he had inside of him. All the feelings he couldn't form into words.

He held her against his body, swept the bottoms of her bikini aside and began to touch her, pushing two fingers inside of her as he kissed her.

She shivered in his arms.

He wanted her. Desperately. More than anything.

This was so foreign to him, and yet it was life as he knew it with Birdie. On this island. It had only been two weeks, and he had forgotten what it was to live in Basilia. To be the king. He had forgotten what it was to care about things other than his own need.

This had been a vacation. The first one he'd ever had.

He had lost himself. And he would have to find himself soon, but not now.

Not now.

He freed himself from his swim trunks, and lifted her up off the ground as he thrust inside of her. He took them both to the heights, standing like that behind the waterfall, nothing but his strength and his desperate need for her keeping them from falling.

Something inside of him burned. He wanted to make declarations. He didn't know what they were. They were wordless, swelling sensations in the center of his chest, and he had no way to translate them.

So he didn't. He simply felt. He simply claimed her. Over and over again until neither of them could breathe. Until their cries of pleasure reverberated off the walls in the cavern, overtaking the sound of the waterfall.

Then he gathered her to him, carried her back to the

house, and up the stairs into the bedroom that they were both sharing now.

He tucked her against him, pushing her hair back off her face.

"You really are incredible," she whispered.

"What did you like about me?"

The question sounded small. It sounded desperate, and he couldn't say that he liked the sound of it on his lips, but he couldn't hold back either.

"I like the orgasms," she said, smiling up at him slyly.

"No. Not now. Before. You said you thought you loved me once."

"Oh." She took a deep breath. "I didn't know you. You were a symbol of something, I suppose. Someone who had power, but who treated people well. I felt like you would take care of me. I let myself spin fantasies around that, even though I knew that it would never happen."

"You took care of everyone else. You just wanted someone to take care of you."

She nodded slowly. "I suppose that's it."

"How do you do it?"

She wrinkled her nose. "How do I…?"

"You're very brave, Birdie. Unlike anyone I've ever known. I've been appalling to you, and yet you treat me with kindness. You have stood your ground every step of the way, even though all the people in your life sought to lower you, you wouldn't kneel."

"I did plenty of kneeling while I scrubbed the floors, Your Highness."

"I don't mean that. Yes, you did scrub floors. Yes,

you worked at the palace, you did work for your step-mother, but your spirit was never broken."

Right then, he felt like a crack had opened up in his chest. He felt like perhaps something was broken in him, and he desperately needed to know what might fix it. Desperately needed to understand what might heal it. Put it back into place. Except he wasn't sure when it broke, or what had caused it. He didn't know what the source of it was, or how to mend it. Didn't even know how to describe it.

"Because I didn't choose any of it," she said. "I remember having the thought very early on… You know, so many people turn to drugs or alcohol or other self-destructive behaviors to handle the kind of abuse that I went through. I don't judge them. I can't judge anyone for how they cope with the sort of life I had to live. And many people have been through much worse. But I remember thinking that I wasn't going to let my step-mother decide how happy I was going to be. I wasn't going to let her ruin my life. She already had too much. I wasn't going to give her everything. My mother wanted to see me happy. I know she did. She told me, before she died." She looked up at him, her eyes glittering. "I remember going into her hospital room, and it was so scary. There were wires and monitors everywhere. She was in the bed, she looked so not like herself. She was gray and so thin. And it terrified me. But she told me that she had everything she ever wanted in life, except for more time. She had a good life. Even if it was too short. That she loved me, and that she wanted me to be happy. More than anything. That she wanted me to smile, for all the smiles that she wouldn't have. To watch the sunset, for everyone she wouldn't see. To dance, because she couldn't anymore. She didn't want me to live for her, she made that very clear. But she wanted me to live. To appreciate each and every moment, and I try to. When I feel overwhelmed, I pull away from everything, and I just feel the breeze. I feel my breath. I feel being alive. That's how I do it. It's why I keep going. It's why I breathe. Now I get it. I'm having a child of my own, and I get it. Because no matter what, I want this child to be happy. To smile all the smiles that I missed, and to dance every time I couldn't. And now I want to be strong for that child. Here. For as long as I can be. I want us to do better for our child than was done for us, and it isn't that my father didn't love me, but I do believe that he was irreparably damaged by the death of my mother." She paused.

"That's another thing. My father let all that pain drive us apart. But we are here. Alive. We could've been close. But he threw himself into work. I never wanted more money. I never wanted a bigger house. I wanted a hug from him. I wanted more time with him. The greatest gift you can give your child is yourself. Your attention. Your affection. That's exactly what we should do for our child. And it's another reason to cling to that resilience that I found."

God, she was strong. Brave. She saw a world filled with miracles. Small moments. Deep breaths.

He saw a sword, hanging from a thread in the throne room. That at any moment it could fall.

That was how life felt to him. A series of cruel, unfortunate events waiting to befall anyone who had the temerity to care too much. Anytime he'd been tempted to believe in miracles, he'd been brought crashing back down to earth.

The line holding that sword aloft felt more tenuous than ever.

"Tomorrow we have to go back."

She snuggled against him, burying her face in his chest. "We're going to be together. It doesn't have to change."

CHAPTER FOURTEEN

She knew immediately that it was going to change. But she'd try to remind him anyway. But she had sensed the subtle shift in her husband's behavior as the end of their honeymoon had drawn close. But of course, the palace was the site of so many terrible things for him. Here on the island he had been buoyant. Carefree. On the island, it had been like he was a different person. But she could feel a heaviness to him once they boarded the plane to take them back to Basilia.

It lasted the entire flight, and when they arrived back, she felt it settled in her own breast.

It was a strange thing now, to be going back to the palace unified with him. Sort of.

She took a deep breath, and pasted a smile on her face for the walk inside. Princess Emerald was there, along with Andrei. And Elizabeth.

She rushed to Elizabeth, and threw her arms around her. "It's so good to see you."

"Good to see you too." She looked at her, her expression filled with concern. "Are you well?"

"I'm quite well," she said. Smiling. Because she could. Because she was here with Onyx. Because even though he was a difficult sort of man, he was a wonderful one.

And they'd had great times, and undoubtedly, would have some difficult ones coming up. Because that was how life was.

So she was just going to have to deal with it. Get over it. Brace herself for whatever would come, and stay open, because you couldn't protect yourself from pain. Well, you could. You could embrace all that anger, like she'd done before the honeymoon, but it didn't heal anything.

The honeymoon had been healing.

But she had a feeling...

She just had a feeling that he was headed for an absolute crash out, and she was going to have to be ready for it.

Was going to have to be as strong as she ever was.

"Do you think you'll have time to take tea with me this week?" Emerald asked, smiling at her. She hadn't spent very much time with Emerald, owing to the fact that she had been so angry with Onyx.

"I would love to," she said.

If she was going to count her blessings, then having Emerald as a sister was going to be one of them.

Because she knew what it was like to have terrible sisters. Emerald wasn't that. She had been firmly on Birdie's side from the beginning. Standing against her brother when he had brought her in here with all that rage and indignation.

Emerald was a deeply good person.

"I'll make a tea time, then. We can have it in my parlor."

"That sounds excellent."

"I've some work to do," Onyx said, touching her arm.

"Okay," she responded.

She tried not to overreact to that. To the immediate distance he was putting between them.

"Come to the kitchen," Elizabeth said.

"I'd love to," she responded.

"So," Elizabeth said when they had some distance. "Things are going well?"

"Yes. They are. Though, I feel him pulling away. Everything was fine on the island. He…" She swallowed hard. "I do love him, Elizabeth. I fear that I do love him, and it's going to hurt me. Like it always does."

"Life is nothing without love. And it's even less without hope."

"Is that why you never tried again with Adam?"

Elizabeth swatted her arm. "No. It's because I didn't want to take a risk, didn't want to damage my pride. Sometimes you have to be willing to soften yourself. When he can't. I wasn't willing to do that. And I regret it."

"But if I soften myself, I could get hurt."

"Yes. But you'll hurt either way, won't you?"

"I think you're going to have to take a risk."

"Then I think you should," Birdie said.

"Me? I'm old now."

"Elizabeth, I haven't talked much about my mother. But I've been talking to Onyx about her, and it's made it all feel closer than it normally does. She died when she was young. She didn't have the chance to be old and in love. She didn't have the chance to be old at all. Aging is a gift. You being here is a gift. As long as you're here, you should make it the most glorious, joyful experience that it can be."

Elizabeth put her hand over Birdie's. "Oh, you sweet girl. I know you're right."

"Then I'll be brave. And you can be too."

After that conversation, she went to her room. She wondered if he would come in. But part of her knew that he wouldn't.

The problem with Onyx was that he had spent his life being unchallenged as far as his authority went. He'd had terrible things happen to him. But he was in a secure place. They were things that were beyond his control. So many of the situations that Birdie had been in hadn't been in her control. Even if she had to fight, there was something she could do to make them better, or worse. In some ways, she wondered if that made him stuck. If it made it difficult for him to know what to do. If he was just sitting there, waiting for the next blow.

The idea of that, the image of that, made her so desperately sad.

And that was when she decided she wasn't going to wait for him. That was when she decided it was okay that she was the one that was making the moves. That she was the one deciding on this particular brand of bravery. Onyx was brave. But there were things she understood about herself, about her feelings and about her emotions that she had a feeling he didn't quite get yet.

So she was willing to put herself out there for him. For that.

That was when she decided to use the adjoining doors. They hadn't used those here. And in the Bahamas they hadn't used doors at all.

But that had been a different place. They had been outside of this. Outside of time in a way they weren't now. This was their life. She was going to make it the best she could.

She was going to speak the language he understood. This was how she had reached him the first time. But this time he knew who she was. This time he knew who they were.

And she believed in what they could be.

She moved through the door, and he turned sharply. He was standing by his dresser, shirtless, wearing nothing but a pair of dark slacks.

"I missed you today."

"Sorry. I had a lot of work to do."

She began to strip her clothes off, wordlessly. He didn't turn.

"I spent some time with Elizabeth."

"I'm glad."

She was completely naked then, standing there in the open.

"But mostly I was thinking about you."

He turned then, and whatever he was about to say died on his lips. She was satisfied by the look on his face.

"Here we are. With the lights on."

There was nothing unusual about that, of course. They'd had each other with the lights on, out in the sunshine, any number of times when they were in the Bahamas. But here, here she was making a stand. Making a statement. This had been a palace filled with so many terrible memories. A palace filled with his grief. With her sorrow.

She was wanting to change that.

While they could.

She breathed in. The scent of him, heavy in the air in his room. She looked at the way he drew breath, the shift of his chest, the way his lips parted.

She was entirely in the moment. With Onyx.

There was nowhere else that she would rather be. And no one else she would rather be with.

"Be with me," she said.

"I'm with you," he said.

She shook her head. "No. Be with me in this moment. And nowhere else. There's nothing but us."

She moved toward him, putting her hand on his bare chest, stretching up on her toes and kissing him on the mouth.

She could feel the moment he surrendered. He wrapped his arms around her, drawing her close to him, and she capitulated in return. Opening for him. Softening for him.

Inside, she made a vow that it would always be like this. That she would always do this.

That she would be his, and she would give whatever he needed. Whenever he needed it.

Onyx might have to learn.

That love was worth the risk.

Do you even know if it is?

Maybe not. But she hoped that it was. It was the world that she wanted to live in. The love she wanted to believe in.

He was a good man. He was a good man whose life had been upended by loss and tragedy. And complicated by his position.

His grief around his marriage was so complicated. So much about what they hadn't been, but then also the sudden loss of his wife had affected him. He dismissed it, in conversation, because they hadn't been in love, but she could see that it was another thing that hurt him. That made it hard for him to trust the world. To trust life.

To feel safe with anything.

She moved away from him, reached down and undid his belt, undid his pants, dropped down to her knees slowly in front of him and palmed his glorious cock. Then she leaned in, testing the length of him with her tongue. Before taking him in deep.

He moaned, gripping her hair, holding her fast while she lavished attention on him. She loved this man.

She loved him. She would get on her knees before him like this, to beg, for anything he wanted.

She had said to him on that flight to their honeymoon that she would not be a doormat. She wasn't a doormat. She knew exactly what she was doing. She chose this.

She chose him.

She chose to be brave in the face of uncertainty.

She chose to be strong because she could be. She couldn't lose him. Which was a great and terrible thing.

He wouldn't divorce her. She was pregnant with his child.

Their marriage would never split up, but for her, it wasn't about the marriage. Not about the legality.

It was about the way she felt for him.

It was about the love.

She breathed in, sharp and deliberate, and then continued to pleasure him.

He was lost in it, she could tell. She wanted him to be. She wanted him to surrender to this. To surrender to them.

She wanted everything.

She could feel him beginning to lose control. Feel him shaking and shivering, but he growled then lifted her up off the floor, carrying her back to the bed. Oh, what a luxury for the two of them to make it to the bed. To make it to his bed.

They'd never been together like this here in the palace. He spread her out over the blanket, and then he began to feast on her. Starting at her neck, down to her breasts. Between her legs, where he licked her until she was screaming.

They were both normally so impatient. But he took his time over her. He pushed two fingers deep within her as he began to suck then lick her, until she was crying out his name.

She was lost. There was no sense of time or place. There was only this moment.

His tongue. His hands. His breath. Her heartbeat. Her pleasure.

Him, her. Nothing more.

Her climax crashed over her like a wave, every ripple stealing her breath.

She held onto the blankets, felt the way it was against her skin, curled her fingers tighter, digging her nails into her own palms, and relished that little bit of pain.

Everything had become Onyx and Birdie. And nothing more at all.

She shattered again and again, and when he rose

up to kiss her mouth, thrusting inside of her body on a growl, she couldn't hold back anymore. "I love you."

His thrusts became wild, unmeasured, and it was the lack of patience, the intensity of it, that had her crying out another climax, just as he went right over the edge again.

"I love you," she whimpered. "I love you."

He pulled away from her, his expression fierce, wild.

This was the moment she had been dreading. This was the moment she knew might happen. He was afraid.

"You don't have to say anything," she said.

"I've lost myself in this," he said.

"In what? This marriage? This marriage that you are supposed to have, that you have to have in accordance with tradition?"

"It doesn't have to be like this."

"Were your parents a love match, Onyx?"

"And they're dead," he said. "So what does it matter? What does it matter what their marriage was? It didn't protect them. Nothing protects you in this life. I have to focus on running the country. I cannot be distracted with this."

"You're dying," she said. "What's the point of living when you're actively dying. Because you won't let anyone close to you. Because you need all of these things and you won't let yourself have them."

"I'm just fine the way that I am."

"You aren't," she said. "The man that I met the night of his wife's funeral, he was drowning. The king that I knew before then, he was doing a good job of keeping up the facade. The reason that your marriage to Circe worked is that it allowed you to ignore your emotions. But even you have to admit it wasn't good."

"It wasn't. I know that. I feel sorrow for her, that she was stuck with me for all her short life."

"So you acknowledge that it's not a good way to live. So why don't you do something different?"

"I can't," he said.

"You can't or you won't? Because the man that I met the night of the funeral, he needed this. He needed love. That was what I gave to you, it wasn't sex. I was wrong. I did love you. I have the whole time. I thought that I loved you falsely because you were a stranger to me, but the truth is, it's always been you. Always. There has never been anyone else for me. There has never been anyone else that I loved or cared about. I love you, you foolish man. In every stage and way that I've known you. As the king of my country, as my employer. As my lover, when you didn't know who I was. As my husband."

"How can you love a man that you believe is a snob at his core?"

"I don't believe you are now. What I believe is that you're afraid. Every time someone gets close to you you pull back. Every time. Because you know what it's like to lose people. Because you know how sudden it can be, and no one can blame you for that. No one ever could. But we are about to have a child—

"No. I cannot think about that. I cannot think about any of this."

It was real terror in his eyes now. And of course. Why wouldn't it be?

"My mother was dying for most of my childhood,

Onyx. I can't even imagine what a terrible thing that would be. To know that you weren't going to see your child grow up. To know that you were slipping away. She did it bravely. And she smiled. She loved me, till her very last breath. We have to love. Even not knowing how long we get to do it. Because love is the only thing in this world that is true. Is the only thing that is good. Love is the only thing that is real. All of these other things could go away tomorrow. The castle could crumble into the sea, and the country could be lost to civil war, but I would love you. You could be a king or you could be an accountant, I don't care. It is the man that I love, not the title. It's you. And I believe that you love me. I don't think you did that night we were together, but I believe you were responding to my feelings. I believe you love me now."

"Birdie," he said, his voice rough. "I didn't like that in my marriage we had strife. It's true. But I also never wanted love. It's a distraction. And for me, it's not something that I can worry about. Because if I have to worry about loving you, then I will always worry, and I don't have the strength for it."

"What about your child?"

"Get out."

"Onyx…"

"Leave."

So she did. She gathered up all of her things, and she left. Her heart was breaking. And maybe he would break it fifty more times. For she would be married to him all of their lives. She felt grim and defeated and bruised. She could stop. She could turn around and say she didn't love him after all. She could even threaten him with a scandal. A royal divorce. But she cared about the fact that he was afraid. She cared about his pain. And that meant bearing it. Letting it become her own.

She took a deep, shaking breath, and began to put her clothes on.

She had purpose. She had her child. She would have tea with Emerald this week. She would have meetings about scholarships and cancer research, and other medical programs.

And all the while she would love him. And in the meantime she would smile. Because she was life.

That would have to be enough.

Onyx felt the crushing weight of pain and anxiety shooting through his chest.

What had he just done?

What had she just done?

The truth was, his denial of her love didn't do anything to staunch the horror flooding him.

It was a terrible feeling. This sense that she was so ephemeral. So tenuous. Because she loved him.

Everything he cared about went away.

He was brought right back to when Emerald had been taken at the altar, and even though it had been Andrei doing it, even though they had reconciled, there had been a moment in time where he'd felt like he'd truly lost everything.

Then there was Circe.

Everything he touched. Everything he touched shattered.

Everyone who loved him…

She loves you.

What if you lose her? What if you lose the baby?

The pain was unending. Unbearable.

He wanted to go after her. But he couldn't.

He wanted to go after her, but his pain had them frozen.

So he stayed in his room. And he locked the adjoining door.

Locked her out.

But it did nothing to block out the pain.

Birdie did her best to have a cheerful attitude when she went to Emerald's parlor for tea.

But something about her expression must've given her away, because as soon as she was served her cakes, Emerald looked at her with concern.

"Are you and my brother having issues?"

She thought about lying. But really, there was no point. Life was too short for a great many things. Lying was one of them.

"Yes."

"Let me guess. He's being a hardheaded tyrant?"

"How did you guess?" she asked, trying to smile.

"Because he can be that way. What's going on? Tell me so that I can help you."

She did her best to recap what had occurred, leaving out the intense sex that happened beforehand—out of deference to the fact that he was her brother—but telling her everything else.

"He's such a fool," Emerald said.

"He's afraid," Birdie said. "And I understand. He's had so many losses."

"Yes, but it doesn't give him an excuse to treat you that way."

She thought about it. He didn't have an excuse. But she wasn't looking for one for him.

"I know. He's being…he's truly being difficult."

"He needs to grovel. He needs to realize that what he's doing is wrong. You should refuse to speak to him until he comes around."

Should she? It didn't feel outside the realm of reason.

"It sounds to me as if you've gone to him more than enough times."

"I think that's the exact advice that I would give to a friend," Birdie said. "But I just can't help feeling that…that I can't afford to cling to pride at the expense of what we could have."

"Well, I would hope that I would extend the same grace to my husband. If he were being such a fool. And he's been a fool in the past. Believe me. But now… If he did it now I don't know what I would do."

"You love him. Just like I love Onyx. There is something simple and uncomplicated about that. Yes, making myself available to him makes me vulnerable. If I could get angry, then I could protect myself. If I cut him off, then I could shield myself, but to what end? I want to be with him. I don't want to leave him. When we were on our honeymoon I was the happiest I've ever been. That's what I want. And you know, if I really thought the issue was that he didn't love me—"

"He loves you," Emerald said. "I'm honestly certain of it. The way that he has treated you has been appalling, and the way that he's afraid of emotion leads me to believe that's definitely why."

"Well. Good to know, I guess."

She was willing to go to him. She was willing to fight for him. Just like she was willing to fight her way out of the attic she'd been locked in. She wanted everything.

And she wouldn't settle for the crumbs.

Neither should he.

CHAPTER FIFTEEN

HE WAS HOLDING his breath, he realized two days later. Waiting for something to happen. Something awful. Something unexpected.

Because he didn't trust anything. How could he? When life had proved repeatedly to be cruel. He'd found this passion with Birdie, they were having a child together and he would never be able to keep her safe. He would never be able to keep their child safe. Life could always have dominion over them, the power to crush them at any moment.

He was a king. With all the power in the world, and he lived his life in abject fear.

For his parents had been stolen from him. He'd had to rearrange all his life to be the man the country needed him to be. He'd married Circe, and then she had died too.

There was no magic key. There was no loving enough or too little or just right. People died. They were stolen away with no notice, and there was no throne, no title, no money, nothing, that could change it.

If he was not safe, if the people in his life were not safe, no one was.

It ate at him. Threatened to tear him apart from the inside out.

Yet Birdie had lost. So much. Her parents, just as he had. Her freedom. Her autonomy. She wasn't afraid. How?

He thought of what she had said to him, about her mother.

Her mother, who had known she was dying, and who loved anyway. But then what good was she? Because she had died, and her daughter had been subjected to a terrible life. A miserable upbringing.

She was loved. And that love had made her who she was.

It was astonishing. Miraculous.

And she had said that she loved him. He'd turned her away.

He was filled with regret.

He was no stranger to the harsh cruelty of life, but… he didn't know what to do when he was caught between his fear of the cruelty, and being the cruelty.

Little Birdie, the maid he'd taken no notice of for so long, was braver than a king. She knew how difficult life could be and yet she didn't flinch.

From the moment she'd found herself pregnant with his baby, she'd been braver, more honest, more forthright, than he'd ever been.

Birdie was miraculous. If there was a key to living, then she had it.

If there was a way for him to heal, it might be through her.

And he'd pushed her away.

He was filled with regret. Loathing. Despair.

How could he fix it?

How?

How could he…?

Could he risk himself? His heart? His hope?

What was the point of being a king? She was right; he had snobbery in his soul. He had treated her appallingly because she was a servant and he was royal, and yet she was the one who was so much higher than he was.

She was the one who put him to shame.

Driven by that realization, he went to unlock the door that adjoined their rooms, and found that the knob was already turning.

He freed the lock, and took a step back, and the door opened wide. There she was, a determined look on her face.

"What are you doing?" she asked, her brows knitted together in angry defiance.

"I was coming to get you," he said.

"You were coming to get me?"

"Yes."

"Why? You don't want me. You don't… Just go away and leave me be."

She was shutting him out again, and she had every right to do it. He'd been awful to her when he'd first taken her from her stepmother's house and she'd turned away from him then—which he'd rightly deserved—and he deserved it now.

But he needed her to give him another chance. He needed it.

And the only way to get one was to risk himself. His heart. His soul.

The only way to have her was to cut himself open, to stop protecting himself from the dangers of life.

The only way to have her was for a king to lower himself before his servant.

And so he would.

"Birdie," he said. "You terrify me."

She frowned. "I do?"

"Yes. In ways that I can't explain. That night when you came to me, it was the most passionate, incredible night of my life. It shouldn't have been. It was a reminder to me of how unwieldy being human is, and I find that terrifying. But I couldn't forget you. I had that ball because I had to find you. Because I knew that you were special. Because I knew that I needed you. And then, when I discovered who you were, I used it as an excuse. Because it was too intense. Because I'm afraid. I'm afraid that the sword that is dangling above my throne room will drop at any moment. I'm afraid that everything I love will be lost to me. Because life is so brutal. It is so cruel. But you aren't. In spite of everything, you aren't."

"There are so many things that we don't get to choose," she said. "But I would choose to love you every time. What a gift that we get to have this. What a gift that we can be together. I don't know for how long. Because I don't understand life. I can't see the future. But I know that we are nothing short of miraculous. I know that we can choose to be together, choose to smile, for every day that we are blessed with."

"And our child will learn the same," he said. He shook his head. "I never understood. Our first duty does have to be to our child. Because it's love, not duty that teaches you how to live. Truly. I made so many mistakes in the name of duty. But I have never made a single one in the name of love."

She smiled. "No. You haven't. I love you."

"I love you," he said. "I have since that first night."

"But you didn't even know who I was."

"My soul knew yours. The rest didn't matter. But now that I do know you, now that I know all of you, I am beyond grateful for everything we are."

"I think this is actually how you break generational curses. By choosing to live anyway. By choosing to love anyway."

"Then let me say this one true thing. We will live happily ever after."

EPILOGUE

THE NEXT ROYAL wedding at the palace in Basilia was for a cook and a driver, and it was attended by everyone who loved them.

Including, of course, the king and queen.

And their children.

Onyx and Birdie's oldest was walking now, and was a charming terror who lived to give his father daily anxiety. He was a brave boy who was often pretending to be a fearsome dragon, and threatening to eat anyone who was hapless enough to cross him in the halls.

Their daughter was still brand-new.

As a family, during the reception, they all got up to dance. Onyx held his little boy's hand, and cradled his daughter in his other arm, his wife standing across from him, laughing.

They danced every chance they got. They smiled every day.

He had learned to live in each and every moment he had with Birdie. She'd taught him that.

King Onyx of Basilia was no stranger to the joys of life. That it was beautiful and often vibrant and full of love.

As long as one chose to embrace it.

* * * * *

Loved The King's Until Midnight?
Find out where it all began with
Princess, Pregnant, Prisoner,
the first instalment in Millie Adams's thrilling
Young, Hot and Royal trilogy!

CHAPTER ONE

"So, it's to be a loveless marriage, to a stranger in a strange land."

Princess Emerald of Basilia stared up at her older brother, King Onyx, his gaze dark and uncompromising as it ever was. And then to his left, at her brother's right-hand man, and her bodyguard, Andrei Ardelean.

He might as well have been carved from stone. He was a man who exhibited little emotion, unless you knew him. And Emerald and Onyx were two of the very few people who knew him. Sometimes, Emerald could even get a smile out of him. But not today.

"If you wish to look at it that way, Onyx," she said, staring her brother down, her rebuttal to his attempt at making her decision sound unhinged obviously irritating him.

"It is not how I *wish* to look at it," he said. "It is how it is."

"And what other *solution* do you see? King Lucian asked for me."

King Lucian, ruler of Alabria, The Sea Serpent of the Mediterranean. The most feared, loathed and reviled ruler in the string of islands that made up the Jewel Belt.

"You are my sister, you are not a political bargaining tool."

"Sadly, Onyx, I am. That's what it means when you're born into royalty, and you know that. We have to do what is best for the country. There is no other choice."

"There are many other choices."

"King Lucian is liable to bring his fleet of ships to our island and raid the place to take me."

Andrei shifted where he stood, his black gaze menacing. "He is welcome to try." Even after all these years of living in Basilia, he retained hints of a Romanian accent.

His parents had been fleeing a crime family, so the story went, and they had stowed away on a boat bound for Basilia, but it had sunk and they'd drowned.

Andrei was the only survivor.

He'd washed up on shore, and it had been her mother's and father's natures to take him in like he was their own. That poor, lonely orphan had become a symbol of the welcoming nature of their country. But she knew it had never really been about that. It was about love.

It was only after that that her father and mother had been killed in a car accident, and her brother Onyx had ascended the throne at the age of sixteen. Andrei had been part of the family by that point. Onyx had appointed him as her personal bodyguard, and so he had become her shadow, wherever she'd gone. The three of them were bonded together by loss. By trauma, and she could understand the pushback from them now. But both of them were far too pragmatic to behave this way.

They weren't *children*. Not anymore. They had to put

away their fantasies of this place, being separate from the world and being their own personal haven.

They knew better than that. Onyx knew better than that, whatever he said. He himself was in a loveless marriage with a woman who didn't care for him at all. Emerald and Andrei both hated to see it, and Onyx wouldn't hear a negative word against his queen. Because he had chosen her for reasons of diplomacy. Nothing else, and that mattered to him more than anything. She understood that it was hard to watch your sibling take less than what they deserved, but she also understood why he'd done it. Ultimately, she respected him for it, because he was serving a greater need, a greater good.

That he didn't see her as worthy of doing the same spoke to the fact that however much he tried to pretend that he saw her as an equal, he didn't. It infuriated her. They were royal, they had a duty to their country above all else. Above all notions of love, passion or even personal happiness.

Her mother had given up everything she'd ever known to marry her father, and that marriage had united a kingdom.

How could Emerald do less? In honor of a mother who was no longer here, but who had shaped her in every way that mattered?

She decided to tell him as much.

"What's good for you is good for me. What's good for the future of the country is what I must do, just as you did when you married Circe."

"Don't speak ill of my wife. Do not compare her to a maniacal authoritarian."

"The rumors about King Lucian are simply that. Rumors. We don't know that he killed any of his wives."

"Even if he killed one of them, it's a wife too many. And anyway, they seem to always meet an end, don't they."

"There were only two. He's hardly Bluebeard."

"And this also isn't *A Thousand and One Nights*. You're not going to be able to tell him stories and keep him from doing what it is homicidal maniacs do."

She decided to ignore her brother's hysterics. She'd already reasoned out all of this. She'd been going over the logistics of an alliance between their countries for the past year. She'd first made contact with King Lucian six months ago, via email, and while he was difficult and mercurial she didn't think he seemed like a psychopath.

Though, maybe good psychopaths hid it well. She couldn't know for sure, and she felt it didn't benefit her to be complacent, but if she really felt that she was signing herself up for murder she wouldn't be doing it.

She believed him, ultimately, that what he wanted was an alliance.

Alabria was isolated, had very few alliances with anyone, and would make an excellent trade partner and military ally.

It was just that Lucian wanted marriage in exchange for those things.

She was a good negotiator. She always had been. She could think of no reasonable excuse to deny him what he was asking. There would have to be a better political prospect on the table, and currently, there wasn't.

So she'd agreed to the marriage.

It was signed. Notarized. Official.

Onyx's objections to it meant nothing.

Legally.

They meant something to her personally. But what she wanted personally wasn't the feature here.

She was a princess. With that came an obligation to duty and legacy. That was what mattered to her.

"The agreement that he sent over is very reasonable, and does not have a hint of homicidal ideation. The fact of the matter is, this is a great proposition, a boon for our country, and you know it."

"I don't like it. In fact, I would like to forbid you from doing it."

"Don't. We agreed that I wasn't going to be treated like I was inconsequential because I was younger, and a woman. I am one of your key political strategists and have been for years. I am not your spare, Onyx."

"Of course not. You never have been."

"Then let me do this. Alabria is the gateway to the Jewel Belt of the Mediterranean. Being able to move through that route freely would change the economy of our country. Alabria is bigger than we are. *He* is more powerful. I know you don't like to admit that there is any man on earth more powerful than you, but there is a point where ego becomes foolishness."

His lip curled, his offense apparent. "This is not about my ego, it is about your safety."

It was only then she let herself look at Andrei. His eyes burned bright with a sort of black flame that made her feel a world of things she didn't want to feel. That made her feel…

There was regret in taking this marriage offer, of

course. There were so many things she hadn't done. So many things that she wanted that… They were impossible, and they always would be.

There was, in addition to regret, relief.

Relief that she would get the distance she'd never been able to manage before. Relief that she would be safe from *this*. The tyranny of desiring what she couldn't have.

Even though her brother loved her very much, she would always have had to make a union that mattered politically. Always. She could understand why he was opposed to this, but even if it wasn't King Lucian, it would be another king here or there, a noble, a prince. Someone who could provide a beneficial alliance to Basilia.

"What are your thoughts on the matter, Andrei?" Onyx asked.

Of course he would ask Andrei. His adviser. The chief of his guard. His best friend.

Andrei shifted. "I don't like it. She could be putting herself in danger. I will not allow that."

"You are not in charge of me," she said. "Your job is only to protect me in the situations that I put myself into."

"Andrei will go with you," Onyx said.

"Excuse me?"

She couldn't imagine anything worse. She could not be followed into her new marriage, into the country by… She couldn't. The way that Andrei made her feel, the things that he aroused inside her…

Those were secrets that she kept locked down deep. For so many reasons they were impossible. They always had been. If her brother'd had any idea that she was lusting after the man sent to protect her, then he would no longer be her protector. He was like a brother to them, or rather he was supposed to be. The problem was, he had never quite felt that way to Emerald. At least not after she began to understand why men and women were different, and what made a man beautiful.

Andrei was beautiful.

He had black hair, deep olive skin and a perfectly sculpted face. The cheekbones and jawline of a model, but the ruthless intensity of a warrior. He was a puzzle. For no matter how long she knew him, she would never be able to get entirely down to the depths of him. He was a code that was impossible to crack. If somebody could have, it likely would've been her or Onyx. Given as long as they'd known him. But there were certain things he never spoke of, and emotions that he never showed.

He'd been sixteen, like Onyx, when the king and queen had died. Emerald had been twelve. She had been certain she'd seen tears glistening in his dark eyes that day, but he'd never spoken of it.

He'd never shown his emotion openly.

Even when he'd been a boy, lying in bed, just waking up to discover his parents were dead, his manner had been stoic. Grave.

It was his way.

But he hadn't left her alone in her grief. He'd held her while she wept, maintaining his own solid strength while she dissolved. Onyx had been the king, and while he'd been there for her as much as he could be, he'd been consumed with managing a whole nation rocked by the death of its monarchs.

Only Andrei had been able to concern himself singularly with her.

Theirs was a bond that defied words. And beneath that bond were feelings in her that defied what was possible.

"Of course I will," he said. "I will be a nonnegotiable addition to this envoy."

"But you live *here*," she said, panic rising inside her. "You can't uproot your entire life to follow me to another country."

"My service to the Crown is my life, Princess. Whether that service takes place here or in Alabria is of no consequence. You are my mission."

He was always doing things like that. Always undermining the emotional connection they felt they had with him. Always making it about duty and honor and his place. He wasn't royal, that much was true, but he was their friend. To her, he was a great deal more, whether he would ever know that or not.

Whether he would ever admit it or not.

You are my mission.

If he were any other man, it would be easy to take that as a declaration of some kind. But Andrei just meant that literally. She was a mission. A task for him to see to.

And he was ruining this. She needed to be away from him. She needed an ocean between them, a potentially psychotic husband between them. She didn't fear Lucian, because she'd gotten to the point where being near Andrei was the real source of her fear.

How long could she bend before she broke?

She was hoping to never test it.

"This is ridiculous. He's not going to make a political alliance with us and then *kill me*."

"I will assess the situation," Andrei said. "With your permission, Your Highness, I will send a missive to the Crown and let them know exactly what the princess will require as she evaluates whether or not she truly wishes to enter into this union."

"I've already agreed," Emerald said.

"And we shall add stipulations," Onyx said.

She threw her hands into the air, rage, desperation and her own throbbing heart making her lose control. "God spare me the interference of relentless alpha males."

She meant that in the most derogatory fashion possible.

Storming from the room didn't really help her case. She was trying not to be childish. But she had brokered the deal herself. It was a triumph of international relations. She was throwing herself on this altar, a sacrifice for the greater good of the country.

Well. That was exactly what Onyx was objecting to. But he didn't have the right. She wasn't weak. She knew that her duty was to the country. She knew where they were having difficulty, and she knew where she could make things better. Easier. King Lucian was the most difficult ruler spread across all the islands in this little belt of countries and principalities. She could tame him, then she could help everyone.

She remembered her mother, so beautiful and serene. She truly believed that her parents had loved each other, but she also knew that her mother had left a small village on the farthest end of the island that previously hadn't been joined together with the nation of Basilia. She had united the tribes there and the rest of the country. Had brought services to them. Had changed the lives of everyone for the better.

She wanted to be like her mother. She wanted to do something that mattered. Wanted to unite the nations. She had the opportunity to do that on an even grander scale.

It was her purpose.

What she knew about life was that it could be short and cruel. Even if she did meet her fate at the hands of King Lucian, she would've tried. Would've tried for a legacy that was bigger than herself.

The need to be her mother's daughter in this way was an almost desperate drive inside her. She'd lost her so long ago. This felt like finding a connection to her.

I'm the woman you would have raised me to be. If you had lived.

She heard heavy footsteps behind her, and she didn't even have to turn to know who it was. Her brother walked on top of the floor. He was silent. Years of royal training had turned him into an elegant panther. Dangerous, certainly, to some, but smooth. Andrei did not bother to conceal his presence, ever. He was a blunt instrument. A weapon. And he wore that proudly.

"You are making a mistake," he said.

She turned around, trying to steel herself for the impact of him. Even though she had just been looking at him, she knew that he would make her heart beat faster now that they were alone. Now that he was closer. She turned, and she was right. Her heart leapt into her throat like it was trying to escape. "That's not for you to decide."

"Perhaps not, but I'm telling you all the same."

"I am a princess," she said. "And you are nothing. You would do well to remember that." She immediately regretted those words the moment they came out of her mouth. She didn't mean them. But she was angry. Angry at these men for undermining her. Angry at Andrei for making her feel things that were so at odds with what she knew she needed to do.

It was the worst of both worlds. Not only was her plan being hijacked by the most controlling men she knew, but she wasn't getting the reprieve from Andrei she desperately needed.

She didn't look at him again. She refused.

She was going to prepare herself for the sea voyage to Alabria. King Lucian did not allow flights in or out of the country, unless they were his own. Everyone, including the citizens of the country, had to travel elsewhere by boat if they wished to fly somewhere. It had always been rumored that it was a show of strength. A way that Lucian let everyone know that in his country he even owned the sky.

She didn't care what it was. She wondered if the ship's journey would deter Andrei.

That made her feel guilty too. But she didn't ask, and she didn't look back.

She had made her decision. Whether her brother and Andrei supported her or not didn't matter. She was selling herself into marriage.

It was a choice that only she could make. And she had made it.

* * *

"You could forbid her to go." Andrei was leaning against the doorframe, rage churning in his stomach.

Emerald was being a fool. Very unlike her. She was the most devoted, levelheaded person he knew apart from Onyx. This was a rare miscalculation on her part, but it was one.

King Lucian was a monster. The very idea of that man laying claim to her...

He could not bear it.

"Certainly, I could. And then what? Lock her in the dungeon? You have met my sister. She is the smartest person I know. Smarter than the two of us combined when it comes to matters of negotiation and the economy. The trouble is, it is a very good deal that she's brokered."

"Fuck the deal," Andrei said. "What does it matter? If her safety is compromised..."

"She is also right about the fact that it has never been confirmed he is responsible for the deaths of his previous wives."

"They're also all dead," Andrei growled. "So they can hardly testify."

Emerald was the most precious thing in his world. He would kill for her. Die for her. Whatever was required of him. His devotion to her was complete.

He had cared for her, looked after her from the time she was young. This family meant everything to him. When he'd been taken into the palace he'd seen love for the first time. Real love that wasn't filled with trip wires and toxicity. Unconditional, beautiful love like they wrote about in stories and songs.

He'd loved his parents, because he knew nothing else. He'd loved his parents because he didn't know children shouldn't see violence—passionate or otherwise. He didn't know a father shouldn't strike his son, or expose him to the dark, twisted dealings of a criminal empire. His father had often showered him with praise, and that had made up for the times when being in his father's sphere was hard.

His own concept of love, of family, was so perverted that he'd been completely undone by the purity of the royal family.

It had changed something inside him, and he'd sworn an oath in his own soul to protect this family with everything he was.

He and Onyx were blood brothers. After Onyx's parents had died, Andrei had cut his palm, and Onyx had cut his, and they had shaken hands, solidifying their connection to one another. Emerald was something else. *His*.

And yet he knew that she wasn't. She never could be.

His desire for her was anathema to him. He did his best to shut it off, to push it down, to push her away. He'd been put in charge of her after the king and queen had died. He'd been made her personal guard—though he'd been young. After all, Onyx was king at that same young age, in charge of an entire country. Andrei had ruled over Emerald's safety. He had protected her physically, and had been there for her through her grief. She had become the person who mattered most to him in all the world. A connection that was not familial, but felt soul deep in a way he would never have been able to put to words.

Then it had changed. The intensity of the feelings had always been there, but then that intensity had become deadly. Like a knife resting flat on flesh for years, suddenly twisted so the sharp edge sunk in, deep and terrible.

The great and terrible hunger that had taken over him during a dance at her eighteenth birthday party. An innocent touch of her hand against his and he'd been undone. The fierce need to claim her, to make her his, to take her until they were both breathless…

It had dogged him now for six years, this deep caring that had turned into something so much more obsessing.

He exhausted his sexual energies elsewhere, faceless, nameless hookups that he found shameful in the broad light of day, especially when he looked at her.

But there was nothing that could be done. He was not angry now because she was marrying someone else. That had always been what was destined to be. He was angry because this man, this mad king, could put her in danger.

"This is why you need to stay with her. Obviously if you think there is any real danger to her safety, I expect you to put a stop to things. Start a war on your way out if you have to."

Andrei crossed his arms. "I'm listening."

"You will gather intel for me. You will tell me everything, about the king, about the country, about the palace. If we have to have an international incident, then we must. If you think that he will be unkind to her, abusive in some way, if you believe that it is a place she will not survive, then at any point during the marriage, you will remove her, bring her back."

"I promise."

"I know that I can count on you. I have trusted you with my sister, and her safety since she was fourteen years old. I continue to trust you now."

He smiled, but it was not a genuine smile. Because if he had any idea that Andrei's feelings for Emerald had begun to change years ago, when she had begun to look like a woman, and her sweetness, her care had gotten beneath his skin in a way that no one and nothing else ever had, he would likely have Andrei thrown in a dungeon for the rest of his life. Beheading would be too good for him.

"I'm sorry about the boat trip," Onyx said.

Andrei shrugged. Yes, he felt cold terror in his veins when he thought about going out on the water. When he thought about what it had been like when the ship had begun to take on the ocean, until it was more water than boat. The way that the pressure of the sinking vessel had pulled him down, and the way his lungs had burned as he had swum endlessly in the wrong direction. How he had washed up on the shore, he couldn't say. It was a miracle, he had decided. Because there was no other explanation. But every other man, woman and child on that boat had died. And so, he had always found it to be a sharp-edged miracle. Because if the divine had saved him, then surely the divine could've prevented the boat from capsizing in the first place.

He had a long-standing rift with God over that.

"It is nothing," he said.

Because when it came to the choice between his own comfort and protecting Emerald, he would choose her every time.

And so he would choose her now. Above all else.

If he had to lead her into this marriage that she had chosen, he would.

And if he had to cut her husband's throat to save her, he would do that too.

The one thing he would never do, was put his hands on her.

Get up to 4 Free Books!

We'll send you 2 free books from each series you try
PLUS a free Mystery Gift.

Both the **Harlequin Presents** and **Harlequin Medical Romance** series
feature exciting stories of passion and drama.

YES! Please send me 2 FREE novels from Harlequin Presents or Harlequin Medical Romance and my FREE gift (gift is worth about $10 retail). I may cancel anytime by emailing ReaderServiceInfo@Harlequin.com or by calling 1-800-873-8635. If I don't cancel, I will receive 6 brand-new larger-print novels every month and be billed just $7.19 each in the U.S., or $7.99 each in Canada, or 4 brand-new Harlequin Medical Romance Larger-Print books every month and be billed just $7.19 each in the U.S. or $7.99 each in Canada. That's a savings of 20% off the cover price! It's quite a bargain! Shipping and handling is just 75¢ per book in the U.S. and $1.75 per book in Canada.* I understand that accepting the free books and gift places me under no obligation to buy anything—they are mine to keep for free no matter what I decide.

Choose one: ☐ **Harlequin Presents Larger-Print** (176/376 BPA G3CD)   ☐ **Harlequin Medical Romance** (171/371 BPA G3CD)   ☐ **Or Try Both!** (176/376 & 171/371 BPA G3CE)

Name (please print)

Address   Apt. #

City   State/Province   Zip/Postal Code

Email: Please check this box ☐ if you would like to receive newsletters and promotional emails from Harlequin Enterprises ULC and its affiliates. You can unsubscribe anytime.

Mail to the **Harlequin Reader Service:**
IN U.S.A.: P.O. Box 1341, Buffalo, NY 14240-8531
IN CANADA: P.O. Box 603, Fort Erie, Ontario L2A 5X3

Want to explore our other series or interested in ebooks? Visit www.ReaderService.com or call 1-800-873-8635.

HPHM2603